Praise for *Puddles*

Lovers of soap operas and women's fiction will surely enjoy and appreciate Lynn Barry's perceptive capture of a mother-daughter relationship and struggle to understand, love and appreciate each other in PUDDLES.
—Andrew Neiderman, author of THE DEVIL'S ADVOCATE and other novels.

"It's a page turner that is at times racy without being vulgar, funny without being ridiculous, and sweet without being sickening."
—Marvin Bartlett, author of *The Joy Cart*, and a FOX anchor person.

"This short, entertaining book leads readers into the struggle for identity in the midst of personal turmoil, while managing to capture the triumph of the human spirit."
—Jenny Ahn, reviewer for Syracuse New Times

"What Ms. Barry has here are a few slices of the real world revealed."
—L.A. Johnson, reviewer from Midwest Book Review, and the author of *The Grass Dance* and *The Alley of Wishes*

"She is an exceptional energetic storyteller."
—Sherry Russell, book reviewer and author of *Conquering the Mysteries* and *Lies of Grief*

"A heartfelt story that will tug at your heart string."
— Victoria Taylor Murray, author of *Thief of Hearts, Forbidden, Friendly Enemies*, and *Le Fin, The Lambert Series*

"This book offers humor, a little mystery, and an entertaining look at how one woman deals with her life which seems to have turned into a soap opera."
— Christy Tillery French, book reviewer and author of *Chasing Horses* and *Wayne's Dead*

"This story has a dark humored approach to a simple life being turned upside down."
— Kathy Bosworth, book reviewer and author of *Your Mother Has Suffered a Slight Stroke*

"Being a man I was surprised to find myself sympathizing and even identifying with Susan as she struggles to understand her friends and family."
— Henry Custer, author of *Concept of Justice* and *Dirt Floor*

"*Puddles* is a book in the form of a soap opera, and the author has faithfully followed this structure from start to finish."
— F.E. Mazur, author of *Spine*

Puddles

by

Lynn Barry

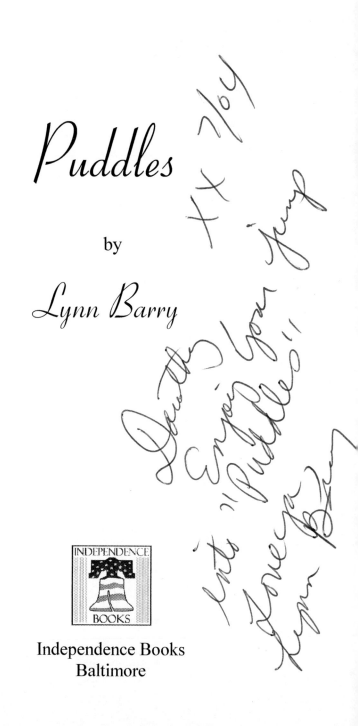

INDEPENDENCE
BOOKS

Independence Books
Baltimore

Dorothy

Enjoy your jump

into "Puddles"!!

Love ya

Lynn Barry

xx 7/04

Second printing

ISBN: 1-58851-139-1 _____
PUBLISHED BY INDEPENDENCE BOOKS
www.independencebooks.com
Baltimore

Printed in the United States of America

Dedication

Dedicated to my parents,

Ray and Ethel Axelson,

for teaching me about faith,

tolerance, forgiveness,

and unconditional love.

As parents they are as close to "perfect" as parents can be.

Acknowledgements

Tom for loving me forever,
Ben for being my "writer" child to love,
Patrick for being my "singer/songwriter" child to love,
Star for being my "puddle jumping" child to love, and Brad
for being my "special surprise" child to love.
You are the greatest family.

DeeDee for being the greatest sister,
Jim for being the greatest brother,
Janie for marrying Jim,
Ken for marrying DeeDee,
Mom and Dad Barry for bringing Tom into the world for me to
love forever,
Bradford for being the greatest brother for Tom—we miss you,
Nicole for marrying Ben,
Adam for marrying Star,
Emily, Jessica, Caseylynn, Elizabeth, and Hunter for being the
greatest grandchildren.
And Alison, Ryan, Noah, Heidi, Aarron, Madi, Zoie, Josh,
Erin, Jake, Jason and Eric.
You are the greatest people to be related to.

And for the following: Debbie McKurth, "Dreams do come
true," *The Patriot* for publishing my articles and column for
several years, The Creative Writers of the Southern Tier for
early feedback on *Puddles*, The Writers of Fillmore who meet
at the Wide Awake Club Library for their enthusiastic support
of my writing successes, and a special heartfelt thanks to
PublishAmerica, Inc. for making my dreams come true.

Chapter 1

"I wake up every morning and say, I'm not going to yell today!"

"All right Susan, what's she done this time?" Maryann asked.

"Let me put the tea kettle on before I get talking about my darling daughter. Would you like lemon or…?"

"Lemon's fine."

"I guess we just don't get along," complained Susan.

"And now that Jeff is out of town during the week and Max is away at school, it's really obvious. Jeff has always gotten along better with her. You've noticed, haven't you?"

"Yes, I have. So what did she do this time?"

"Natalie came home this afternoon after track practice all smiles, telling me that Johnny and Beetle splashed her in the puddles. Then she said that she got them back by running around splashing them, too. And get this, she said it was s-o-o-o-o fun!"

"That's it?"

"Well, yeah," Susan answered. "She's fifteen years old. I can't imagine why she'd get so excited about running through puddles."

"I'm sorry," Maryann smiled, "but I think you might be overreacting. What's the big deal?"

"What's the big deal? Come on, you're the neatest, cleanest person I've ever known. You've even washed cruddy dollar bills before." Susan wore her displeasure on her face.

Maryann pushed her chair back and got up. The teakettle whistle blew as Maryann left the room. Susan poured herself a lonely cup of lemon tea. They were good friends who avoided confrontation.

Beetle scooted into his apartment to get cleaned up. Natalie had gotten him good. The muddy water seemed jet propelled when it had come to his turn to get splashed.

"What the hell happened to you?" Beetle's mother Judy snapped. She was short on patience and understanding when it came to raising a teenage son on her own. She was glad that some of the older kids let him hang around them.

"Don't worry about it Ma. I'm gunna get cleaned up. Remember, I'm goin' with Mr. Swanson to the Y?"

His mother softened. She remembered. She also remembered how wonderful it was that "The Mr. Swanson" had taken an interest in her son. And he's not bad lookin' either, she thought.

"No, I didn't forget. Now you remember to ask him in after." Judy's body was in great shape from walking. She kept her hair long.

"Ooh Ma, you got the hots for old Swannie boy?"

"Shut up! Beetle!"

Gordon Swanson straightened the desks in his sixth grade Science room. He loved to have the rows in order so the janitor could do a good job sweeping.

"I can't wait to take Beetle swimming at the Y. All those God damn fathers who don't act like fathers!" he grumbled out loud. At dinner Susan stared at her cleaned up daughter. You're not going to yell she repeated over and over in her mind.

"So, you feel better, dear?" she asked.

"I didn't feel bad." Natalie gave her mother one of her

pouty lipped, rolled eyed looks.

"Well, Would you like cheese on your spaghetti?" Susan posed with a can of grated cheese between her hands.

"God Mom. I never want that."

Relax, Susan coached herself. "Fine, dear. Fine."

Natalie twirled strands of spaghetti around her fork and sucked in an oversized mouthful, then let go a rude slurp.

"Come on, Natalie. Can't you eat right? My goodness, you're fifteen. Haven't I taught you anything?" So there it was. Susan couldn't keep her mouth shut. All the feelings she'd felt that afternoon seeing her daughter all muddy spewed out.

"Get a life, Mom!" Natalie pushed away from the table and took off.

"Where are you going?" Susan pushed backed, too.

"Out!"

Natalie being a track star was no match for her mother. She ran out the back door and over the fence.

Susan's throat closed up. She panicked.

"Natalie, get back here!" The stress knots returned. It scared Susan to see Natalie vault the 6' high fence that surrounded the backyard.

Susan went back to the house to get her car keys. She was going to drive around to find Natalie. Her breathing came in short pants, which gave her little energy or comfort.

"Should I see if Maryann wants to go?" Susan said out loud. "No, this is my problem. I bet Natalie's headed straight for Johnny's," Susan speculated. She drove with one hand in the twelve o'clock position, the other in the nine. She only drove like that when she was nervous.

House after house blurred, until they looked like one long house instead of a block of them.

"Why didn't she like dolls?" Susan had always resorted

to that argument. She'd long ago deduced that Natalie never liked to play with dolls as a child like she had, so therefore that's why they didn't get along. Doll lovers would never enjoy running through puddles.

When she caught up to Natalie, her daughter broke stride. Her breathing came in defeated gulps. She didn't fight it.

"What…do…you…want?" Her fifteen-year-old shoulders jerked up and down, as she labored to control her breathing.

"Get in the car, Nat."

"Why should I? All you ever do is put me down."

Susan felt a lecture surfacing, but stifled it.

"Oh, Natalie. For heaven's sake, I'm your mother. Mothers are supposed to care enough to lecture and correct and yes, criticize." Susan waited; hoping it would be an acceptable explanation.

"Well, maybe you shouldn't care so much!" Natalie started towards the passenger's side.

They returned to the house in silence. Susan wanted to give her daughter a good smack and then hug her until their bodies tired, but did neither.

Natalie scaled the stairs, as soon as they arrived home. She'd always run to her room. Susan didn't try to stop her.

"I hate it!" Natalie yelled. "I want to take off so bad!"

"Sometimes I wish you would run off," Susan mumbled.

Natalie talked softly to Johnny on her bedroom phone.

"I hate it," she complained to him.

"You want to sneak out and meet me?"

"No, I'd better not. But how about ditching school tomorrow?" Natalie knew he'd want to. He'd been pressuring her to do that for months.

"You mean it, Nat?"

"Yes, I do."

"Beautiful," he said.

Natalie met Johnny after first period. They carefully walked out the door near the gym that goes out in the back of the school and is not visible to teachers and administrators patrolling the halls and grounds. They slipped into the woods holding hands, feeling the thrill that some people feel when they do something they aren't supposed to.

"We did it, Nat. I can't believe it. What made you decide to now?" Johnny asked.

"What difference does it make? It's what you want, isn't it?" Natalie knew what was coming. Johnny would want to "do it." She was nervous.

They walked another hundred yards, before they dared stop. They found a spot that was completely sheltered with a circle of bushes. Johnny took his jacket off and laid it on the grassy area in the center of the circle of bushes.

Johnny fumbled with her heavy sweatshirt, awkwardly pulling it up over her lacy bra.

Johnny barely slipped off her jeans and panties before wanting to enter her.

Natalie closed her eyes, and waited.

Johnny kissed her mouth hard as he worked at penetrating her. She struggled a little at first, but then gave in.

Chapter 2

Maryann loved her job as lab technician at the Lambson Research Laboratory. She examined a variety of specimens, from blood samples to bones. She found the work fascinating. The benefits were good, too. She'd worked there for twenty years, and especially looked forward to the school tours. It was an opportunity to be around kids. Today, there was a group of sixth grade Science students visiting.

"Good morning, Mr. Swanson," she greeted. He'd been bringing his Science classes to the lab for years.

"Hello Maryann," he returned with a semi-wink, and an almost flirty smile. "Excuse me class," he said to his students, and ushered Maryann to the side of the room. "Would you like to go to dinner with me tonight?" he whispered.

He'd caught her cold. In the ten years that he'd been coming there, they'd joked around, chatted about scientific breakthroughs, and had a kind of friendship, but never an actual get together or date.

Maryann felt uncomfortable, but heard herself agreeing.

"Well, sure why not."

"Great. Can I meet you here after work? What time do you get off?"

"Four o'clock."

"That's perfect."

Susan daydreamed while doing the breakfast dishes. She remembered the day she'd brought Natalie home from the hospital. Jeff was in love with his little girl. Max wasn't sure about his new sister, and she was recovering from the reality of having to have a c-section that time.

The phone rang, which interrupted her daydream.

"Hello?"

"It's me, Maryann. Have you got a minute?"

"Sure, Maryann," Susan felt a little awkward after the night before visit, "Hey, sorry about last night…"

"Oh, don't worry about it, I was tired, or…I don't know," she sounded like she felt awkward, too. "Let's just forget about it."

"Well, what's up?" Susan asked. Maryann had never called her from work. "Is something wrong?"

"No, actually something's right. I've got a dinner date."

Susan had never known Maryann to have any kind of date, so this was new, "A date? That's great."

"Yeah, you must know him. I'm sure your kids had him. It's Mr. Swanson, the sixth grade Science teacher."

She'd known Gordon for years through the school. She wouldn't have pictured the two of them together. But then she couldn't picture either of them with anybody. They were the types who were never with anybody, so it seemed normal for them. Susan was thrilled for her friend, who she'd assumed would go to her grave an old maid.

"Yes, Susan, Gordon Swanson." Maryann always called her Susan when she was dead serious about something. "I was wondering if you could let Fluffy out. We're going from here after I get off work."

"Of course, but are you going in your lab coat?" Susan teased. "Or would you like me to bring up some clothes?"

"No that's okay."

"Just kidding, Mar."

"You're so funny."

"Will you be out all night?"

"Very funny. No, I'll call you when I get in."

"Oh good. You know with Jeff away I need juicy scoops to live on."

"Oh stop it! You watch too many soap operas. Give Fluffy a kiss for me."

"That's where I draw the line." Susan said. "I don't kiss dogs."

"Thanks Sue. Gotta go back to work. Bye."

To work, Susan thought. She'd been putting off going out of the home to work for twenty years. How can I be this content at home by myself, she wondered? Hey, be glad that you are, an inner voice spoke to her.

Susan finished doing the dishes, wiped down the counters, took out the garbage, and went to Maryann's.

"Fluffy," she called out. She's a yippy thing, and sure enough she charged at Susan yipping in full voice.

"It's okay, girl. Your mother asked me to check on you."

Fluffy wouldn't shut up. Susan was tempted to snoop around. She walked down the hall to Maryann's bedroom. It was immaculate, as was the rest of her small home. She spied a framed photograph on her dresser. Susan wondered who she was.

Susan couldn't ask her about the photo because she'd have to admit she'd been snooping. She walked out of the bedroom, feeling ashamed of herself. Fluffy yipped louder, as if to rub it in. "Oh be quiet." Then Susan let her out, which was what she'd come to do.

After she returned home, she decided to write a letter to her first born college boy Max, which usually helped her vent her frustrations with Natalie. He had little patience with Natalie, too.

Dear Max,

Here's the latest. Your sister is into running through puddles. Isn't that charming?

Susan didn't fill the entire letter with that, but it was enough to help her let go of it. "Today is a new day," she said out loud.

Then the phone rang. It was the school.

"Is your daughter Natalie at home today?"

"At home, no. What do you mean? She's at your school."

"It seems that she went to first period, but no one has seen her since."

The school has a strict policy of calling parents when students aren't in class, and not absent.

The bad feelings Susan had moments before written away in a letter to Max, flooded back like a major dam had broken.

"You've got to be kidding," Susan was furious. "Can you tell me if a Johnny…" but before she could say his last name, the woman from the school office said, "Yes." Most people at school knew about Natalie and Johnny.

"Thank you for calling. I'll look into this."

Before Susan could breathe, or think of tracking her daughter down and shooting her, she dialed Jeff. She didn't like to upset him during the day. She supported his decision about trying the job of principal, after years of teaching, even though it meant being gone during the week. She felt good about running things by herself, but she needed him, now.

"I'm sorry, Susan. Your husband is away at a meeting, all day." Jeff's secretary was a twice-divorced woman in her thirties. "Can I help?" she asked. "Or did you just want to talk?"

"You know, if you have a few minutes, I would.

"Sure."

Susan used up those few—plus minutes complaining about what she was dealing with at home. Jeff's secretary listened, until she had a call on another line, and had to go.

What am I going to do? Susan wondered.

She had the urge to snoop through Natalie's room like she had at Maryann's. This time she didn't feel the least bit guilty, though. Maybe I'll find a clue as to where she is, she thought.

Clothes were strewn across the floor. The bed wasn't made, and there was dust on every piece of furniture. Susan insisted that Natalie clean her own room, which meant it didn't get done.

"For Heaven's sake, Natalie." She opened drawers, found folded notes, read them, and refolded them. And then she found a condom underneath a pair of socks.

"Why did I have to find this?" Susan shoved the drawer shut. What is going on with her, she wondered?

Susan decided to get in the car, and try to find Natalie. She didn't think she'd be able to, but she had to try. Susan didn't know what she was going to do with her daughter, though, if she did find her.

"Skipping school is an all time low. I'm so embarrassed."

Susan shook her head in shame. The daughter of a school principal should not be skipping school. What did I do to make this happen, she wondered? As a Super Mom type person, Susan always blamed herself.

She remembered when Max was caught shop lifting, and how she had agonized over that for months, until Max had said, "Mom, don't be so hard on yourself. You are a good mother. I just screwed up." His words had helped her at the time.

Susan was delighted that Max was doing well at college, but at times she really missed having him around. They had a special bond. She wished she could say the same for Natalie and herself.

Susan tried the school grounds, the mall, Johnny's house, and the bus station. She wondered if they had run off together. "I'm being silly," she laughed nervously, trying to calm herself. When she arrived home, Natalie was sitting in the kitchen having a PEPSI.

"Where the heck have you been?" Susan said.

"At school." Natalie didn't look at her mother.

"Well, the school called and said you weren't. What do you have to say about that?"

"I was at school." Again she wouldn't look at her mother.

"Natalie Lee, where have you been?" Susan shouted. "I know that Johnny wasn't in school either."

Natalie bolted from the room.

"Get back here, I'm not through with you!"

Susan was no match for her daughter. Natalie was in her room with the door locked, before Susan reached the stairs.

"Open the door."

"Leave me alone, Mom." It sounded like Natalie was crying.

"I can't take it, Natalie. I don't know what I'm going to do with you. I can't believe you skipped school. What the hell is going on with you?" And there she did it. Susan hated to resort to using swear words. She had never heard her parents swear, and was determined to not use them, either. But then they didn't have Natalie, she did.

Susan sat outside her daughter's door for awhile, occasionally pleading with her to come out. Natalie kept refusing.

Then Susan said, "Natalie, I have to go to Maryann's to let Fluffy out. She has a date."

"She has a date?" Natalie finally spoke.

"Yes, with Mr. Swanson."

"You're kidding."

"No, I'm not."

"That's weird."

"Why don't you come out, and go with me. Fluffy likes you. And then we can talk."

Nothing happened right away, but then the door opened.

"Okay, let's go." Susan held back what she wanted to say, saving it for after they took care of Fluffy.

Natalie had a mean look on her face as they walked to Maryann's in silence. Natalie let Fluffy out. The little ball of fluff leaped at her, happy to see her.

"Hi, Fluffy, sweetie." Natalie snuggled the dog to her cheek. "I've missed you."

Susan found herself feeling jealous. It seemed to her like Natalie never missed her or wanted her around.

"Better put her down so she can go."

Natalie rolled her eyes, and sighed with displeasure. "I am, Mom. Can't I love her first? Is that a crime?"

"Don't get me started, young lady." Imaginary fumes blew out of Susan's nostrils. "You are in big trouble."

As expected, Natalie put the dog down and headed for their house.

"Yeah, go ahead and run away." Susan had wanted to

talk to her, but this was okay. She figured she'd talk to her at dinner. At least Natalie was running home and not somewhere else.

Fluffy yipped non-stop at Natalie.

"You're a big help," Susan scolded her.

She put Fluffy in, and got to take another look at the photo in Maryann's bedroom. It was in a black wooden frame. It had a date on the back.

"Hmmmm, this is twenty years old. The woman looks like she may be in her late teens, but it's hard to tell." Snooping again reminded her that she'd have to confront Natalie about the condom. She didn't care if Natalie knew she'd been snooping.

"Good bye Fluffy."

The dog yipped.

Susan's steps matched the throbbing in her head. There'd be no getting away with this, she resolved.

She pushed open the back door, took a big breath, and summoned her daughter with her loudest voice.

Natalie strolled into the room with a finger in her mouth. She had a nail-biting thing at times.

"I am not proud of myself, but I looked through your room after the school called," Susan paused, "and found a condom."

"I can't believe you looked through my stuff."

"You're missing the point."

"That's my room!"

"This is my house!"

"Fine!"

"So what about the condom?"

"What about it?"

"How can you talk like that? Didn't I raise you better?"

"Oh Mom get a life. This is the nineties. Condoms are no big deal. Aren't they supposed to save lives and all that crap?"

"Natalie, when I was your age I was still playing with my dolls."

"Well, I'm not you. And I wouldn't want to be, anyway."

She'd succeeded in ripping her mother's heart out, and Susan still didn't know where Natalie had been all day, and why she had a condom.

"What do you really want to know, Mom?" Natalie gave her mother a disgusted look. "Do you want to know if I've had sex?"

Oh Lord, Susan choked. Is she really going to tell me? "Oh, Natalie. My dear Natalie, if you're trying to shock me, don't." This time Susan was the one to leave the room.

Susan knelt beside her bed and folded her hands in prayer. "Dear Lord, what am I doing wrong?"

Susan meditated for about ten minutes, laying her head on the bed, while still kneeling beside it. She was tense, exhausted, and very concerned about her daughter. She tried to pray every day, but sometimes forgot to.

She heard Natalie walk to the bathroom. Susan started to get up, but then she heard the sound of the bathroom door shut and the click of the door lock. She lay down on her bed, and continued to pray.

"Father, I need help with Natalie. I believe she may be sexually active, and I don't have a clue as to how to handle her. I try to talk to her and end up getting mad each time. Please help me Lord."

Susan closed her eyes and worked at taking deep breaths. She also tried yoga once and utilized the breathing methods to aid in relaxing. Soon she'd fallen asleep and the reality of her problems took a break for the day. Dreams came quickly to her and they were peaceful. The nightmare was over until she had to wake again.

Chapter 3

Natalie slid into the tub of warm bubbly water. She felt strange about "doing it" with Johnny. Thoughts of being in the woods like she and Johnny had been, reminded her of the days she and Max used to go hunting with their dad. "I miss you Dad." She ducked under the foam.

Jeff read his secretary's message. "I wonder what's going on." He didn't want to call. He had so much on his mind. The new job was often more than he was able to manage. Living away from Sue and Natalie during the week was difficult, at times almost unbearable.

It isn't right, Jeff thought. He was disillusioned and overwhelmed, but he didn't want to admit it to his family. He knew what a hard thing it was for them to be away from him, too. At times the guilt he experienced over taking the job was immense. He wanted it to work.

"If I don't call, they'll have to work it out. Sue and Nat have to find a way to get along." He blew out a long breath. "I think I'm doing the right thing. I can't take on one more problem, even if it is my family."

He left the office to go to the health club he'd joined to unwind before having a lonely bite to eat in front of the TV at the boarding house he lived in during the week.

"Hey, Boss!" his secretary called after him. Jeff had noticed the way she looked at him. He knew the type. Her looks often said, "If you want me, I'm available." He'd seen it from others before.

Those looks, he hated to admit, were beginning to drive him crazy. But he loved his wife, and would never want to make a mockery of their wedding vows. Still, he wished she wouldn't tempt him.

"You off to the health club?" She was doing it again.

"No, I'm going to buy my wife a present. She really misses me." Jeff lied; hoping the mention of his wife would give her the hint. Her perfume wafted in the air, doing a number on his will power to resist her obvious invitations of wanting him. "Why does she have to be so appealing?" he asked his conscience.

"Want company?" she twirled a strand of her shiny long hair around her finger.

"Um," Jeff desperately wished she wouldn't pursue him. He glanced at his gold band around his left ring finger and held firm. "No thank you, I'll see you tomorrow."

The Cracker Tin had nightly specials. That evening it was chicken and dumplings.

"What looks good to you?" Gordon asked.

Maryann felt comfortable with Gordon, even though she'd had little experience with dating through the years.

"That special looks good to me."

"Well, the special it is." Gordon tried to be as charming as possible. He was fascinated with the specimens Maryann got to work with each day at the lab. He was hoping to get her to let him get a closer look, maybe even take pictures.

Maryann wondered if she could be interested in Gordon. He wasn't bad looking, she thought. She wondered if he found her at all attractive. Maryann noticed that men never looked her way. She'd accepted that. She also realized how badly she wanted a child. She was almost desperate. Maybe this is God's way of forgiving me, she thought.

After they'd been served their specials and took a few bites, Gordon thought about sleeping with Maryann. I'll make myself do it if it'll get me into that lab, he thought.

Maryann daydreamed at the table. This dating stuff isn't so bad, she thought. Gordon is pleasant enough, but could I possibly make myself have sex with him, she wondered. Thoughts of babies came to her. I'd do it for that, she thought.

"Well, are you enjoying the chicken and dumplings?" Gordon asked.

"Yes, I am."

"Beats eating alone, doesn't it?"

"Yes it does, but I don't eat alone, actually."

"You don't, what, uh…do you live with your parents, or something?"

"No, my dog."

"Oh, dog…great! What kind?"

The moments left in their first date were filled with Maryann's chatter about Fluffy.

"Can we do this again?" Gordon asked.

"I'd like that," Maryann answered.

"Why didn't you bring him in, Beetle?" Judy griped to her son. "I'm not getting any younger, you know."

"Ma, you're gross. He's my old teacher."

"But I'm lonely," Judy twirled her long hair in a knot, and shoved a pin through it to hold it in place. "Does he have a girlfriend? I know he's not married."

"I don't know." Beetle chugged milk from the carton.

"Hey guess what? Johnny and Natalie skipped school today. I bet they 'did it,' too."

"You don't mean Natalie, as in that teacher or principal's kid?" Judy undid her hair as quickly as she'd put it up.

"Get outta here, really?"

"Yup."

"Woo hoo!"

"She's cool, Mom. I wish she were my girlfriend. The only social life I have is swimming with Swannie boy!"

"Well, if you'd set me up with Swannie boy, maybe I could work at getting you and that Natalie together. What do you say?"

"Forget it, Ma. She'd never be interested in me. You've seen Johnny. And I'm younger, anyway."

"Well, maybe I could get Johnny away from her."

"Shut up Ma. Don't be a pig!"

"You know I'm a fox." Judy struck a sexy pose.

"Oh yeah, Ma. You're a fox."

"Think about bringing Swanson in the next time, don't forget."

"Sure Ma, whatever turns you on."

Susan wondered why Jeff had never called. She knew his secretary must have told him. She was too efficient to forget. Susan understood his wanting to try being a principal, and always supported his every want, but hated being apart from him during the week.

Dinner was quiet. She'd heated up leftover spaghetti, and remembered to not offer cheese this time.

"How are classes?" she asked Natalie.

"Fine."

"Do you have any homework?"

"No."

"Okay."

The spaghetti stuck in Susan's gut all evening. Natalie stayed in her room. Susan stayed away. Susan told her daughter that she would talk to her father about a punishment for skipping school when he returned on Friday.

"I can't wait to see Dad," was all Natalie said.

"I can't either," Susan agreed, and wished she didn't have to.

Susan was doing the crossword puzzle in the newspaper, when Maryann called. "Can I come over?" Maryann asked her.

"I'd love it."

Susan put the teakettle filled with fresh water on the stove. Maybe this time they'd actually get to drink a cup together. A hot cup of tea with Maryann always put Susan in a better mood.

Upon opening the door she noticed a difference in her friend immediately.

"Did you have fun?" Susan asked.

"It's funny, you know I did."

"Come on in. What kind of tea do you want?"

"Whatever you're having."

"It's spearmint, then."

They padded to the kitchen, eager for each other's company.

Maryann filled Susan in on the details of the date, then surprised her friend.

"You must know that I've always wanted a child," she said.

Susan smiled approvingly at Maryann. "I didn't know that. But by the way you seem to love kids, it's not all that surprising when you think about it." "I'm not saying anything will come of this date, but Gordon is nice."

Susan felt sorry for Maryann's not realizing her desire earlier. But Maryann was still young enough to be able to conceive, so what's the difference, she thought.

"You mean you're thinking of Gordon as a potential father for a child you might have?"

"I guess."

"Well, this must have been some first date."

"You know what they say? Still waters run deep." Maryann giggled with her sweet, melodic sounding laugh.

"No dates for years, and bingo. She's ready to hop into bed with the first guy."

"Oh come on, now. Be kind." Maryann sat for a moment then displayed a rascally smile. "Do you think he'd be any good in bed?"

"Well, listen to you," Susan loved it when they joked. "I don't know about this Swanson guy," she offered. "I guess he loves kids, though."

"I can see that he does when he brings his class in for tours."

After they'd exhausted that subject, Susan told her what she'd been going through with Natalie since they'd last talked. The tea water was hot, so she poured them each a cup. The spearmint aroma filled the air.

"Would you like me to take her shopping, "Maryann offered, "like I used to? Maybe she'll talk to me."

"You could try. I don't know if she'll go, but if she does, I'd appreciate it. I'm past desperate with her," Susan confessed.

When the tea was gone in their cups, and the time was right to end their visit, Susan leaned in to give her friend their traditional good bye hug. She always felt Maryann needed hugs, living alone like she did.

"Better rest up for your next date," Susan teased. "Who knows, maybe you'll go off for a weekend."

"Oh you...stop it! You're terrible." Maryann giggled.

"You do have a point, though. I probably shouldn't

waste any time."

Susan looked Maryann dead in the eyes, and said, "I was kidding."

Chapter 4

Beetle jogged fast to catch up to Johnny. He would have crawled through mud to catch up to his idol.

"Hey, man where were you yesterday?" he grabbed Johnny's sleeve.

Johnny yanked his arm free. "Lay off the clothes, man…it's none of your damn business."

"Ah, come on Johnny. Everybody knows you and Natalie skipped. So did you guys 'do it'?"

Johnny kept on walking with no expression on his face, until he exploded into a hearty laugh, and said, "Well, what do you think, dork?"

Beetle joined in the male bonding chuckle, slapping Johnny on the back, and saying, "All right bud…you're the man."

Johnny turned, grabbed his arm, and threw him into a head lock position, causing Beetle to squeal. Beetle loved it. Then Natalie showed up, and spoiled the male moment.

"Johnny," she called out coyly.

Johnny released Beetle.

"Hey Nat," Beetle greeted her with a wide grin.

"Hey Beetle."

"I didn't see you yesterday," Beetle asked Natalie.
"Were you sick?"

Johnny gave Beetle a look that said, "Shut up or you die!"

"Gotta go guys," Beetle said, "catch you later."

Natalie spoke under her breath. "I can't believe we skipped school. My mom freaked out. Did the school call your house?"

"I don't know. My ma didn't say nothin'," he acted distant. "Oh, for Christ's sake. I gotta get to class. I'll see ya." Johnny walked off. Natalie trailed behind.

"You listen to me, Johnny." She didn't know what to say. She felt strange around him since they'd had intercourse.

"Don't I get a kiss?"

"Yeah sure," he stooped to kiss her quickly.

"I love you."

"Love ya, too."

They parted. Natalie felt like there was much she needed to say. Johnny was anxious to get to gym class and play indoor soccer.

Maryann decided to take the initiative this time. She called Gordon's school, and left a message to have him call her.

Work went slowly until he returned her call.

"Maryann, what's up?" he greeted.

"I was hoping we could get together again."

"Oh, sure. When?"

"How about tonight?" she said. "You could come to my house for supper, and meet Fluffy."

"Fluffy? Oh yes your dog. Well, I have a swimming thing I do. But what about after that? Is seven thirty okay?"

"Seven thirty is great. Do you like lasagna?"

"Oh my, lasagna. I sure do."

"I'll see you then."

"You've called me from work twice in one week," Susan teased her friend. "That's a record."

"I know, and I can't talk long. I was wondering if I could ask a big favor?"

"Sure, what is it?"

"Could you pick up a frozen lasagna from Sandy's Gourmet Shop? I'll pay you later."

"Hmm, Does Gordon know you don't like to cook?"

"Susan, come on. We only had one date."

"I know, but the way you're going, I thought he was close to moving in."

"Very funny. Will you be able to get it for me? And put it in my fridge? I'll pay you later."

"Of course I will. Anything for love."

"Thanks Sue. You're a dear."

Susan did the dishes, pulled a comb through her chin length hair while checking out her reflection in the bathroom mirror, something she seldom did. "Not bad for a woman my age." Her hair had several strands of gray filtering through the black ones. Her figure was a little on the plump side, yet shapely. "Jeff loves me just the way I am," she said. She couldn't imagine worrying about dating, like Maryann. And was glad she didn't have to.

Then she remembered that she was angry at Jeff for not calling, "Oh, Jeff." She missed him more each week, but was relieved that it was Friday, and he'd be home.

As Susan walked down the street to the shop, she thought about Gordon and Maryann. He's a nice man, she thought. He's a good teacher, likes kids, and is single. Maybe this will be good for my friend. Sometimes she wondered why Maryann had never married or dated. Maybe she was holding out for Gordon.

Once in the Gourmet Shop she continued to ponder. Sandy broke her train of thought. "Can I help you, Susan?"

"Um, yes…a frozen lasagna, please."

"What size?"

"Enough for two adults."

"Oh, is Jeff back?"

"No, this is for Maryann."

"Oh, I see."

"She has a date."

Sandy had been supplying Maryann with frozen entrees for years, and was a friend, too.

"You're kidding."

"No, I'm not."

"With who?"

"Do you know Gordon Swanson, the Science teacher?"

Sandy thought for a moment, "Oh yeah. My sister's kids had him."

"Well that's who."

"Hmm, that's great. I'm happy for her. Always wondered if she was lonely, haven't you?"

Susan wasn't sure how she felt about Maryann being lonely, but went along with Sandy, and said, "Oh yeah."

Susan paid for the frozen lasagna, and slipped out to go to Maryann's to put it in her fridge. Yippy Fluffy seemed almost sociable this time.

Susan marveled over Maryann's neat refrigerator. Everything was perfectly lined up. It made her feel like going home and straightening out hers, but she knew she wouldn't because it was almost time for her soap operas to start. She loved her soaps, always had.

Susan wanted to take one more peek at the picture in Maryann's bedroom, but when she peeked in, it wasn't there. She panicked to think that Maryann knew somehow that she'd been snooping, and had hidden it from her. Oh well, she thought, I'll never mention it. After all, she's the one who wanted me over here with her gone. It's really her fault.

Susan laughed at herself for being so ridiculous. The woman's face in the photo was permanently photographed in her memory, anyway. Some day it'll come up and it'll be no big deal, probably a distant cousin, she figured.

Before Susan left though, she noticed the photo was set up in the living room. Curious, she pondered. Now she could ask her about it.

The soaps filled her afternoon, until she decided to make a beautiful dinner for Jeff's coming home night, a nice pot roast with potatoes, onions, carrots, and baby peas. She dove into the preparations, figuring they might as well have good food to eat while they discussed Natalie. She knew Jeff would have good ideas. After all he was an educator, he was supposed to know how to handle kids.

When Natalie came home from school she seemed to be in a good mood. "Hey, Mom," she greeted with that "hey" thing Susan hated, but which she ignored in the interest of getting along.

"How was your day?" Susan asked.

"Fine."

"That's good."

"Did Dad call?"

"No, but he'll be home soon."

"Good."

"You miss him?"

"God yes."

"Me, too."

Natalie opened the refrigerator, and grabbed a handful of grapes. That pleased her mother. Susan usually had to nag about eating fruit to Natalie. Susan smiled. Natalie smiled back.

"Friends?" Susan asked.

"Friends," Natalie agreed.

"You know I only want the best for you?"

"I know Mom."

Relief spilled over Susan like a warm rain shower. Maybe there was hope for them after all.

"Can I call Max?"

"Your brother?" It was unusual for Natalie to want to call her brother. They'd never gotten along very well.

"Yeah." Natalie waited.

"Well, sure. Tell him I said hello."

Natalie left the kitchen, to call him in her room.

Susan was curious as to why Natalie wanted to call Max, but pleased.

Plopped down on her bed, with her brown hair hugging her shoulders and her face set in an anxious expression, Natalie dialed Max's dorm room number.

The sound of his voice calmed her, she was glad he was in. "Hey, Max. It's me, Natalie."

"Oh, hi, Sis. What's up?"

"Just wanted to call."

"Really?"

"Well, I kind of have some questions, but you gotta swear you won't tell Mom."

"What's going on?"

"Johnny and I did it."

"You…"

"Yeah."

"Gee, I don't know what to say. What do you want me to say?"

"Nothin', I just wanted to tell someone, I guess." Natalie had heard that Max was experienced, and wanted to let him know that she was, too.

"Natalie, I'm real uncomfortable with this. Can't you talk to Mom about this?"

"Are you crazy?"

"Well, she and I have had talks about sex." Max waited.

"But she likes you better than me, and don't say she doesn't!"

"Natalie, shut up!" Max lost it. "If you can't talk to Mom, then talk to Dad."

"Maybe."

"I gotta go." Max's awkwardness caused him to want to end the conversation.

"Fine. That's the last time I call you."

"I wish you didn't feel that way, but if that's the way you want it." And then he added, "Be careful little sister."

"Yeah right!" Slam, she hung up.

Chapter 5

Beetle raced Mr. Swanson in the water. Their strokes were perfectly matched. They took breaths at the same time. When they surfaced, Swanson gasped. He had a good feeling about this kid.

"Hey, Mr. Swanson, do you want to come over to my house after we're done swimming? My ma said it was okay." He didn't want to disappoint his mother, and he wanted him to come over, too.

"Well, I would, but I already have plans."

"Oh, that's cool. Maybe another time," he laughed. "I think my mom is interested in you, though."

"Oh really?" Swanson commented as they tread water.

"Well, maybe I should change my plans." Gordon felt like he'd reeled out his line, and snap, he'd gotten a nibble.

"You would?"

"You bet I would. I'll call."

He dried off, changed, and went to call Maryann.

"I'm so sorry, I'll have to take a rain check," he lied.

"That's okay," Maryann answered, but didn't want to let him off the hook, either. "How about tomorrow night?"

"Tomorrow's great. I'll see you then." Two big fish on the line, Swanson boasted to himself.

Beetle called his mother to tell her Mr. Swanson was coming over. Judy was thrilled. She went to her room to change. She doused WHITE SHOULDERS perfume on her neck and upper chest, pulled on a tight fitting lilac sweater, and

41

poured herself into form fitting black jeans. She left her hair long.

The men arrived, and Judy went to work on Mr. Swanson. She wanted a man. She was real lonely.

"Aren't you going out with friends tonight, Beetle?"

"Oh yeah, Ma." He winked at her.

"You're not going to be here?" Gordon asked. "Then I'd better go, too."

Judy quickly spoke up, "Well, now, why don't you stay? I don't have any plans; we'll get a pizza. Would you mind?"

"Not at all," he flashed her a flirty smile.

Beetle went out, they ordered pizza, and threw back the beers, one after the other. It wasn't long before Judy was on Gordon's lap, and they were making out. She kissed him in between drags on her cigarette. When the pizza came they kept on drinking and making out, forgetting about eating.

Maryann knocked at Susan's door.

"What is it?" Susan grilled her upon opening the door. "Do you need to borrow something for your dinner date?"

"No," Maryann answered with sadness. "He canceled."

"Oh."

"Yeah, he said something came up, but he said he'd come tomorrow."

"Well, that's good, isn't it?" Susan wasn't sure if Maryann was having second thoughts about the whole thing.

"I guess, it's just that I was all set for tonight, and tomorrow I might not be."

"You mean you might not be in the mood?" Susan teased.

"You are so bad, but yes, I guess so."

"Would you like to eat with us? Jeff should be here

soon."

"Actually, I was wondering if Natalie would like to go to the mall, and eat. You know, like what we talked about? I might even crack down and get a new outfit."

"No, really? And it's not even your birthday." Susan couldn't resist teasing her.

"Ha ha. You are so funny these days."

"I'll tell you what. I'll see if Natalie wants to. It would be nice to have Jeff all to myself."

"Okay, call me and let me know."

"You bet Mar, I'll catch you later." And then Susan remembered.

"Oh, I don't mean to be nosey, but I noticed a photo of a woman in your living room, and wondered who it was."

"So you were snooping, were you?"

Susan's face flushed at being found out. "No, I…"

"Hey! Gotcha Susan. Oh that's an old friend I used to know. Everyone has photos out; I wanted to be like everyone else. Real dull, huh?"

Dull, no, sad, yes, Susan thought. Maryann left.

Susan went back to the pot roast. The meat was tender; it almost fell apart the way Jeff liked it. She added the peas, and gave it a sprinkle of cracked pepper. The aroma was wonderful. While her back was to the door, Jeff slipped in.

"Hello, gorgeous," he greeted, as he grabbed her from behind. His arms made her dizzy. She fell into him with relief. She could get romantic just hearing his voice.

"Oh, Jeff, honey," Susan spun around to face him.

"How's big Mama?"

"Kiss me, and I'll tell you, you old kook."

They locked onto each other with a kiss they'd perfected over the years. It was better than any she'd seen in her soaps. We could teach those actors a thing or two, she figured.

"Forget the small talk," Jeff said, "right here, right now, baby."

"But we've got pot roast."

"Well, then pot roast, first."

"No, first I'll call Natalie. She wants to see you, and Maryann has invited her to go to the mall."

"When's Maryann going to get a life?" Jeff joked.

"Be nice, actually she's seeing Mr. Swanson, you know, the Science teacher."

"Get out of here, really?" he looked amazed. "I never liked that guy."

"Really? I never knew that. Why not?"

"Beats me. Just always thought there was something not quite right about him." Jeff headed towards the stairs. "I'll get Nat."

"Wait a minute," Susan said, "you never called me back. Let me fill you in on this week, and then we'll get joy girl."

"Oh boy, let me hear it."

After Susan filled him in, he said, "I think no phone use or dating for two weeks would be good. Do you want me to tell her?"

"That sounds good, and yes you can tell her." Susan was relieved not to have to. She knew Jeff would remain calm.

Natalie wasn't happy, but accepted her punishment. She decided she might as well go to the mall with Maryann, since her life was pretty much over for the next two weeks. Once again, Susan was relieved to not have to deal with her for the evening, and have Jeff all to herself.

Natalie wore a large sweatshirt with light blue jeans and black combat boots. Susan didn't say a word. She hated those boots, and Natalie knew it.

"Have a nice time."

"Thanks," Natalie kissed her mother quickly. Jeff was showering, so he missed the good byes.

Maryann greeted Natalie as she got in on the passenger side of her car, "Hey bud, thanks for coming with me. It's been a long time since we did this."

"Yeah," Natalie agreed.

"So what's this I hear about you?"

"What do you mean, has my mother been talking about me?"

"No, well, yes. She told me you skipped school."

"Oh, God, next she'll have it put in the newspaper." The rolled back eyes came next, then the huge sigh.

"You want to talk about it?" Maryann asked.

"Not really."

"Well, I'll listen if you change your mind. And I mean listen, nothing else."

"Okay," Natalie appeared more relaxed. "Maybe." They walked through the mall, had cheeseburgers at BURGER KING, bought temporary tattoos, ate donut holes, and Natalie talked a lot, and Maryann listened.

"So you promise you won't tell Mom about me having sex?"

"Um, yes, I promise, but I think you should talk to her. I'm concerned about you getting pregnant, or contracting a sexually transmitted disease."

"I know," Natalie bobbed her head in agreement. "But It's just me and Johnny, so I won't get any disease, but yeah, the pregnancy thing, yeah, I know."

Maryann felt real uncomfortable about not telling Susan, but good about Natalie trusting her. She lay awake that night wondering what to do.

Susan knew exactly what to do when it came to pleasing Jeff. Twenty-five years of practice and wanting to make each other happy did it.

She caressed his back, and laughed remembering the time he'd asked her if she wanted him to shave the hair on his back, and she'd said, "Are you kidding? I love it."

Then there was the time he thought she liked having her breasts rubbed firmly, and she'd finally said, "This isn't a breast exam, go easy!" He'd laughed so hard; they lost the mood and just snuggled.

That night was wonderful, she'd felt absorbed into his skin during lovemaking.

When Natalie came home, Susan was reading an article in the TV GUIDE, and Jeff was sleeping peacefully beside her. Natalie peeked into their room.

"Hey," she greeted in that way Susan hated.

"Hi Hon, did you have a good time?" asked Susan.

"Yeah, you know Maryann's pretty cool."

"She is, huh?"

"Yeah, we bought tattoos, can you picture her with a tattoo? Maryann the biker lady. So, did I get any calls, even though I can't talk on the phone?" to this she'd rolled her eyes, predictably.

"No, the phone never rang."

"Really?"

"Really."

"Well, good night, I'm so tired."

She approached the bed to give her mother the obligatory kiss.

"Good night, dear. Have a good sleep."

Susan watched her daughter leave the room, and felt

sad. She'd hoped to have a warm, close relationship with her daughter. She remembered staying up until four o'clock in the morning talking to her own mom when she was alive, but they'd had a closeness that she didn't have with Natalie.

"What am I doing wrong? What am I doing right?" She put the TV GUIDE down, and snuggled up to Jeff's back. The warmth she felt with him drew her in. He snorted, and stirred, but didn't wake up. She fell asleep thinking about Natalie.

Chapter 6

The guys had hung out at Johnny's all evening. They'd played video games, eaten chips, and drank JOLT cokes, the kind with lots of caffeine. Beetle told the guys that Mr. Swanson was at his house.

"Are you serious?" Johnny asked.

"Yeah, isn't that cool?"

"Phhhhh." Johnny made a disgusted sound. "I was beginning to think old Swannie boy was gay. You know how he goes around with kids all the time, no dates, no wife, you know?"

"Well, he's at my house, and my ma has the hots for him, that's all I know."

"Hey man," Johnny said. "Don't take this wrong, but your mom is 'hot' for an old lady."

"Man, it's okay, I'm proud of my mom."

"You should be, man."

They got to wrestling around on the floor, as usual. Johnny pinned Beetle easily. Beetle didn't mind. He accepted the fact that Johnny was stronger as well as better looking than he was.

"Let me up," Beetle struggled. "What are you hard up? Man, don't be pretending I'm Natalie."

With that Johnny let go of Beetle. "Shut up, gay wad."

Beetle doubled over laughing. "Besides, why aren't you out with her, anyway?"

"We're not married, you know. I don't always have to

be with her."

"Hey man, that's cool."

"Besides, she doesn't own me. I can go out with other girls."

"Are you crazy? Why would you want to?"

"Man, you are such a baby," Johnny grumbled. "If you don't know, I'm not going to tell you."

Feeling embarrassed, Beetle decided to go home. He'd wanted to check on his mother and Mr. Swanson, anyway.

When Beetle came in, Mr. Swanson set Judy down and excused himself.

"You don't have to leave, Swanson," Beetle said.

"Thank you Beetle, but I'm tired. Been a long day. Your mother is nice. I think we're going to have many more times together, you, me, and your mother."

Beetle smiled. It was what he'd wanted.

"Good night Judy."

"Good night, sweetie," she slurred. "Come again, honey."

When Beetle had seen his mother on Mr. Swanson's lap, he was happy for her. He'd hated his father for walking out on them. "Did you have a good time, Ma?" he'd asked her.

"Sure Beetle. And if you hadn't come home, I might have had an even better one."

"Oh, sorry, Ma." Beetle was used to her crudeness after she'd been drinking. That was the way she was. She flopped onto her bed, ending their mother-son conversation. He put water in the sink, and did the dishes for her. Then he straightened up the room before going to bed.

Saturday morning, Susan woke up refreshed. Jeff was beside her, and then the phone rang.

"Hi Mom," Max's voice surprised her. They talked

Sunday nights, and very seldom any other time, unless there was a problem.

"Max?"

"Yeah, Mom, you probably think something's wrong."

"Well, is there?" Susan's voice communicated her concern.

"Kind of, I was in an accident."

"Oh my God!"

"I'm okay, Mom, just whiplash."

"Oh honey, I'm so sorry. But what happened?"

Max detailed the night before events. A drunk driver had back ended him and a friend of his. Their seats had broken, and they were lying down when it was over. Both were taken to the hospital in an ambulance and had extensive x-rays. Both had suffered whiplash.

"Your father and I will be up in a few hours."

"No, that's okay, Mom."

"But I'd like to see you."

"Actually, I was hoping you would, thanks, Mom." And then he added, "Will Natalie be coming?"

"I don't know."

"Maybe she should."

"Don't tell me you miss her. I thought you two hated each other."

"I don't hate her. I just wondered."

"Well, I'll invite her, but I hate to travel with a grump, if you know what I mean?" Susan said.

"Oh boy, do I ever. I would have used the "b" word, though."

"Rhymes with witch?"

"You got it." Max laughed.

"See you in a couple hours. Love ya."

"Love ya, too, Mom."

Susan woke Jeff up, and filled him in.

"Well, if he's okay, why do we have to go?"

"Jeff, how dare you," she scolded. "Don't you want to make sure he's really okay?"

"Of course. I'm just so comfortable. I was hoping for another round with you this morning." He pulled her under the covers.

"Ohhhhh nooooo, you must be confusing me with your mistress. You know I don't do mornings!"

"Oh yeah, I forgot." Jeff knew she was kidding, but her comment made him a little uncomfortable after realizing that he was beginning to have inappropriate feelings about his secretary.

"Now, get up Jeffy boy," she pulled free. "I have to wake joy girl, and see if she wants to go."

"Ah, let's go by ourselves," he begged, "We can eat out, too."

"Okay, we'll let her have the day off. But can we trust her?"

"No, but I want to be with you." Jeff sat on the edge of the bed. "She's already skipped school. If anything's happened, it's probably already happened."

"Well you've got a point there," Susan said. "Ain't parenting fun?"

"A real blast and a half."

Susan went to Natalie's room to tell her what was going on. She was concerned about her brother, but not overly.

"No boys over," Susan said to her. "You still shouldn't be talking on the phone. And don't go anywhere."

"I won't."

"You can have a frozen microwave pizza. It would be

nice if you dusted your room maybe even cleaned it. And make sure you clean up the kitchen. And hey, it would be a good time to read a book. You used to read a lot."

"Okay, okay, Mom." The eyes rolled again. How Susan hated that.

"I love you, Nat. We'll see you tonight."

"I love you, too."

They did love each other. They'd always known that. It's just that life got in the way of them appreciating each other. Maybe someday, Susan thought.

Susan went to the kitchen to call Maryann.

"So she'll be there alone all day?" she asked.

"Yes, we're probably crazy to let her after her skipping school, but Jeff is desperate to be with me, and quite frankly I'd rather not take her."

"Do you want me to invite her over?" Maryann asked.

"No, you've got your date."

"I'll keep an eye on the house, if that will help?"

"Thanks, that would be great."

Maryann studied her figure in the mirror, after showering. "No chest, no waist, no hips," she said. "I'm not exactly the seducing type, but I still have the equipment, so I guess the packaging isn't the issue." Her desire for a child superseded her self-consciousness. "I'll ply him with alcohol." She smiled at her cleverness.

The doorbell rang, and her cleverness turned to nervousness. She rushed to pull on clothes, and answer the door. Fluffy was having a yipping fit.

"Good evening, Gordon."

"So this must be Fluffy." The dog charged at Gordon's leg.

"Fluffy, get over here!" Maryann commanded. Fluffy

retreated to Maryann's side. "I'll be just a moment." Maryann took Fluffy to the bedroom to confine her.

"I'll put on some music to cover the yipping."

"It doesn't bother me." Gordon walked about the room, as if he was comfortable there. "So, Maryann, I'm dying to hear more about your job. And I was wondering if you could give me a more in depth tour sometime." He wasted not a moment to try for what he really wanted.

"Um, well, I don't know." She was flattered, but eager to set her plan in motion, too. "I suppose, but hey, how about a drink? What do you like?"

Gordon felt a rush inside. He had Beetle's mother interested, which meant more time with Beetle. And now he was getting the old maid interested, which meant a closer look at dead bodies. "Do you have any wine?"

"Red or white?"

"What's for dinner?" he asked.

"Lasagna."

"Then red, please."

They drained the bottle of red wine, while chatting, and dining on warmed up frozen lasagna.

"I feel a bit flushed, could I lay down?" Gordon really did feel flushed, with the combination of red wine and spicy sauce. But Maryann assumed he was being suggestive.

"Oh sure, let me relocate Fluffy." Fluffy had finally stopped yipping. She reconvened after Maryann moved her to the basement.

Maryann showed Gordon to her bedroom. He lay on the bed. "I get this way, sometimes."

"It's okay." Maryann slowly took her clothes off and lay down next to him.

"What's going on?" he said.

"Isn't this what you wanted?"

"Well, okay." He sat up, and took his clothes off, too.

They got under the covers, and Gordon rolled over on top of Maryann. He pushed against her pelvic area for a long time until things were right, then he entered her and he climaxed inside her. She never moved.

Gordon got out of bed, and grabbed for his clothes. "You let me know when I can have that tour, okay? Hey, you make a great lasagna." He looked back for a brief moment, then left.

Maryann laid still. She wanted to get pregnant. She didn't want to disturb the sperm, even though she felt like scrubbing herself until all traces of the man was off her body. "I hope this did it, I don't want to have to do that again."

Fluffy yipped from the basement. It was a desperate cry. It broke her heart.

Natalie dialed again. Johnny picked up. "I've been calling you all day," she said.

"So."

"So, where have you been?"

"What's with the third degree?"

"My parents weren't home all day."

"Oh?"

"Just oh?"

"What do you want me to say?"

"I don't know. I just wanted to talk to you or see you."

"What about now?"

"Never mind, it's too late, they'll probably be home anytime," Natalie complained. "Good bye."

She hung up the phone seconds before they walked in. "How's Max?"

Jeff filled her in on Max, while Susan glanced around,

trying to detect any evidence of unacceptable behavior.

"I didn't have any guys over, if you're wondering, Mom." Natalie had on a smug expression.

"I'm not," Susan lied. "But I'm glad you didn't."

"Probably tried," Jeff teased. He could get away with saying something like that, where Susan couldn't.

"Shut up, Dad!"

They danced around. Susan was amazed at their relationship. They seemed so easy around each other. With Natalie and Susan it was like taking a trip to the dentist just to have a simple conversation.

"Did you talk to Maryann at all?" Susan asked.

"No."

"I just wondered how her date was going."

"His car is over there." Natalie peeked out the window.

"I guess it's going well."

"I hope so. Maryann's such a sweetheart."

Jeff rolled his eyes this time. He was still uneasy about Mr. Swanson.

They made popcorn, and had a family style evening, until Natalie did her, "I'm so tired," routine, and went to bed.

"How can she be sooo tired, if she stayed home all day?" Susan started in again.

Jeff quickly changed the subject. "What do you want to watch?"

"Why can't I ever say anything about Natalie?"

"It's not that you can't, it's just that I want to enjoy the little time I have with you each week. Is that selfish of me?"

It worked. Susan melted. "No, it isn't. Anything is fine."

He rubbed her feet, and sat beside her on the couch, their comfortable bodies molding together like one.

Attending church gave them all an excuse to put away their displeasure with one another, and have a good old-fashioned spiritual time together. Even Natalie loved going to church. They had a youth choir that was upbeat and sang popular songs. The minister usually gave a rousing sermon that was well delivered, and understandable.

"God doesn't make junk!" he called out.

Susan glanced at Natalie at the same time Natalie looked at her. They shared a friendly smile. Maybe there was hope, after all. Susan wondered.

Maryann sat four rows behind them. Susan was anxious to hear how her date had been, but didn't want to think about that now. She was busy thanking God that Max was all right. Susan realized again how vulnerable they all were to having bad things happen to them. Jeff told the congregation about the accident and that Max was okay during JOYS AND CONCERNS time.

As they left the church after the service, she caught up to Maryann. "How was it?" she asked.

"Pretty nice," Maryann lied a little.

"Will there be more dates?"

"I don't know, maybe not," Maryann responded.

"Well, was there a problem?"

"No, I just don't know."

"Did you happen to see anything suspicious going on at our place?" Susan couldn't resist the temptation to ask.

"No, I didn't." Maryann's uncomfortable feeling about knowing about Natalie returned. She wondered if she should tell her about Natalie's confession. Undecided, she kept quiet.

"That's good, maybe there's hope for my Natalie, after all."

Maryann gave a pained smile.

"Want to come over for brunch?" Susan asked.

"No thanks. You enjoy your hubby while you have him."

"Okay, but if you change your mind, come over. Jeff is making eggs, toast, ham and cheese and macaroni, and fruit salad cups. Says he feels like fussing to which I said, "Why not?"

They parted.

"Is Maryann coming over," Natalie chimed in after catching up to Susan outside of the church.

"No," Susan responded.

"Well, then can I invite Johnny?"

"But you're…"

"You said I couldn't talk on the phone, and stuff."

"Oh, ask your father." Susan was good at saying "Ask your father," when he was around.

Natalie found Jeff and got the answer she was seeking. They'd be having lover boy over. "Isn't that wonderful?" Susan commented sarcastically to herself. Once they arrived home, Natalie called Johnny, and she was in luck. He was home, and would come.

"I'll be in the shower," Natalie informed them.

"Couldn't shower for church," Susan complained.

"She's your daughter," Jeff teased.

"Oh no, she's your daughter." Susan threw it back in his court.

"Are you positive of that?" Jeff questioned her.

"Either yours, or that hunk of a mailman's."

"Cute, real cute."

"Well, you asked."

Jeff hugged his wife tightly, knowing that he needed all the reminders he could gather to continue to resist the awful temptation he was feeling lately, to cheat. "I already miss you, Sue."

Snuggled in his strong arms, she agreed, "I already miss you, too."

Life slipped back into the picture, as Susan realized that she had to get his laundry done before he packed up to leave for the week. The hugging had to end.

"Didn't they seem different?" Susan asked Jeff, later in the early evening when he was packing up some of his things.

"Different how?"

"Natalie and Johnny acted differently around each other. Don't tell me you didn't notice."

"Tell me what you mean. Be more specific."

"I don't know. Just forget I said anything," said Susan.

"It's probably me being critical of her, that's all."

"Try to go easy on her."

"And what's that supposed to mean?" Susan was offended by his comment.

"Oh, forget I said that," Jeff shook his head. "You'll do fine."

"Oh, gee, thanks for that."

"Come on, Sue, let's part peacefully. You know how lonely I am down there. I can't start off the week with bad feelings."

"I'm not exactly having a picnic here, you know. I have to deal with her moody majesty."

"I know. I know."

They called a silent truce, and hugged for the last time until the next Friday.

"Have a good one," he said.

"You, too."

As he walked out the door, and then drove away, Susan

couldn't get the suspicions out of her mind. She had a feeling about Natalie and Johnny. And the skipping school business made it more than a possible suspicion to her. She knew she'd have to talk to Natalie about it. She knew she had to for her sake, as well as her daughter's. She would wait until Johnny left and then talk to her.

"Natalie, I couldn't help but notice that Johnny was more physical with you than I've seen before," Susan began.

Natalie cast a mean look at her mother, "What is that supposed to mean?"

"Are you guys having sex?" Susan knew she just had to say it. Pussyfooting around was not her style.

"What the heck?" Natalie was visibly upset with her mother's question.

"Well, are you?"

"No."

"Are you sure?"

Natalie's body language said "yes," even though her mouth said "no." Susan wasn't convinced.

"If you aren't, that's great. If you are, I feel sorry for you."

"Oh God Mom, why are you getting into this right now? Did someone say anything?"

"Who?"

"No one, I thought maybe people were talking junk about me."

"It's a feeling I have, "Susan said.

"You and your feelings. Well, I have feelings, too. I know about AIDS and getting pregnant, and all that stuff." She got teary eyed. "I'm not five years old anymore."

Susan hugged her, and Natalie let her for awhile, before pulling free, and heading for her room.

"I don't believe her, and that's what scares me," Susan mumbled.

Johnny stopped at Beetle's after leaving Natalie's. Judy was the only one home. She'd been drinking beer all afternoon. "You're that Natalie's boyfriend, aren't you?"

"Yeah."

She laughed.

"Is that funny?"

"It is funny that you'd want a girl, when there are women available."

Johnny backed up towards the door. "Um, tell Beetle I stopped."

"Not so fast, handsome." Judy approached him, pinning him up against the door. She pressed her body hard against his, and touched his groin area, massaging him through his pants.

"What the hell?" he groaned.

"Let me," she whispered. "I'm real lonely." She kissed him until he let down any guard he'd put up, and let her have her way with him.

Chapter 7

Monday morning meant one thing for Susan, counting the church's money. She'd been the counter for years. While in the church office, she noticed a poster for a youth weekend away. "I wonder if Natalie would go to that." Susan jotted down the information on a piece of paper, and tucked it in her purse. Susan would love to see her daughter do something besides have sex with her boyfriend, she thought. The image of the two of them having sex made her nauseous.

"Good morning, Susan," the secretary greeted. Cindy was pleasant, and efficient. She had been the secretary for years.

"Cindy, hi."

"Is Natalie going to that?" Cindy had noticed Susan looking at the poster.

"I'm hoping she will," Susan responded. "Are your girls?"

Cindy had twin girls, who were a few years younger than Natalie, named Jenny and Joanna. Natalie didn't hang around with them, but they all knew each other.

"Oh yes," Cindy said. "They go to all the youth group events. I think it's so good for them."

"I hope Natalie will at least think about it. She has a boyfriend, and I don't know, she's awfully preoccupied these days."

"My girls haven't discovered boys yet. I guess I'm lucky."

"You sure are, Cindy. I envy you."

"But Susan," she offered, "It's only natural."

"It's natural, but not easy to be the parent of, when they do."

They both laughed, then Cindy smiled, and Susan fake smiled. Susan wished she were Cindy right then. Girls doing churchy things, no boyfriends. Cindy had it made as a mom, Susan thought.

After spending the morning balancing the money, and stopping at the bank, Susan shopped at the grocery store. Three bags full, her arms breaking, she got through the door in time to catch the ringing phone.

"Hello," she gasped.

"Hey, Mom." It was Natalie.

"What is it, Natalie?"

"Can I go to a soccer game after my practice? It's not like a date, or anything."

Susan hated it when Natalie called from school to ask her stuff. She couldn't say, "Ask your father," this time.

"Gee Nat," Susan stalled, "it's a school night. Don't you have homework?"

"I'll do it in study hall. Please Mom? I'll do anything."

"Anything?" Susan asked.

"Name it, you got it."

"There's this church youth group weekend thing," said Susan.

"Sure Mom, I'll do it, whatever."

"Okay then."

"Thanks Mom."

Susan was so pleased she made a ham and cheese sub for herself to eat in front of the TV. It was soap opera time. THE YOUNG AND THE RESTLESS came on as Susan sat in her comfortable chair.

"Are you comfortable?" Gordon asked his young friend.

"Are you kidding?" Beetle answered. "I can't believe a teacher would let me look at PLAYBOY magazines, this is cool."

"Now, Beetle. You mustn't tell anyone about this. They wouldn't think it was cool. Let's keep this between us." Gordon knew they had to keep it a secret. He'd done this a dozen times before in the past with his young friends. They'd all cooperated.

"Oh sure. I won't say anything."

"You want a beer?"

"Really?"

"Sure, just us men hanging out."

"Yeah, why not. This is so cool."

Gordon felt sweaty. He was close to getting what he wanted. He could feel it. He might not even have to pretend he liked Beetle's mother. It had been so easy this time.

"You are so cold to me." Natalie scolded Johnny at the soccer game.

"Oh lighten up."

"I thought we'd be closer now," She leaned in to him, "You know."

"What do you mean?" Johnny looked puzzled. "Aren't we?"

"It doesn't seem like it to me."

"Oh man, that's it. I gotta go." He pulled away from a reluctant Natalie.

"You jerk, don't embarrass me." She was conscious of everyone watching the soccer game.

"See ya," he called out as he walked away.

Tears appeared in her eyes. "Wait!"

Natalie followed Johnny.

"I think we'd better cool it a little," he said.

"What?" Natalie started to cry.

"I think we are going too fast."

Hearing this, Natalie ran off. She was shocked, embarrassed, and angry.

For whatever reason, Susan had a great time with Natalie that evening. She didn't know why Natalie seemed different. She didn't care. She was thankful. They even talked about Natalie's weekend away with the church youth group.

"Mom. I'm sorry I've been such a bitch lately." Natalie's words were like long-awaited gifts lost in the mail temporarily.

The week flew by. Susan missed Jeff so much she felt faint when she saw him again.

"Hi, big Momma," he greeted affectionately.

"Boy, did I miss you. If you weren't so darn happy being principal, I'd beg you to come back, even if you had to dig ditches."

Jeff grinned. "Well, I'm here now, honey."

"Let's go out. I want to get fish at Barney's. Does that sound good?"

Barney's was the local bar and grill that had excellent fish. They'd gone there often, and had never been disappointed. They always saw people they knew there. Natalie went along, too. She was still grounded.

Once seated, Natalie said, "Dad, I'm going on a weekend thing with the church. Doesn't that sound cool?"

Jeff gave a surprised look, to which Susan smiled happily.

"Hey great. Sounds fun."

"I'm doing good in school, too."

"Excellent. When do grades come out? Soon, isn't it?" they chatted away about school and sports.

Susan busied herself people watching. She saw Maryann in the corner with Mr. Swanson.

Date three was going okay. Maryann wanted to keep seeing him, in case she wasn't pregnant, and had to have sex with him again the next cycle. She found him intolerable after their casual sex episode, but wanted a baby. He found her dull, but wanted that lab tour.

"Could we have that tour tonight?" Swanson asked.

"Tonight?"

"Sure, you must have a key?"

"Well, I do, but I couldn't. It's closed."

"Who would know?"

Suddenly she felt uneasy with his insistence. She excused herself to go to the rest room. While she was gone, he went through her purse, and slipped her set of keys into his pocket. "I don't need the old maid, after all."

"That's funny." Maryann paused at her front door. She had no keys to get in. Gordon had already driven away. He hadn't wanted to come in, had said he was real tired. She walked to Susan's to get the spare.

"Hi neighbor," Susan greeted.

"I can't find my keys. Could I use the spare you have?"

"Of course," said Susan. "Come in. Did you have fun at Barney's?"

"How'd you know?" Maryann looked puzzled.

"Jeff, Nat and I were there."

"You were? Why didn't you say something?"

"I was going to, but I didn't want to disturb date number three." Susan smiled at Maryann.

"Oh."

"Here's the key," Susan handed the spare to Maryann.

"I'd follow you over for girl talk, but Jeff is home and I miss him. Sorry."

"That's okay," Maryann reassured her, "We'll get together soon."

"Swanson didn't want to come in for coffee, tea, or something else?" Susan teased.

"Get into your house," she scolded. "You are so bad."

Susan went in the house. Jeff was reading in bed. She couldn't wait to join him.

The weekend had been too short, as always. Good byes were difficult.

"Could you come down, say, Wednesday night and have dinner with me?" Jeff asked her. "Sometimes I get so lonely." Jeff had been further tested by his seductive secretary, and was praying that he would not fail the test and succumb.

"That's a great idea."

"Oh," the relief in Jeff's voice was obvious.

For the first time, Susan thought about moving. They'd lived there a long time and Jeff had never insisted, but she thought she'd at least think about it.

"I can't wait to see you on Wednesday," he said. Their parting kiss was tender and lengthy. Jeff looked at Susan.

"This kiss has to last me."

"I know," she said. "Me, too."

Later, Susan casually dropped the idea of moving to Natalie.

"There's no way I'd move!" Natalie said. "No way!"

"I didn't say we were," said Susan, who once again grew impatient with Natalie's attitude. "You know, though, if we decided to, you'd have to."

"I can't believe this! Are you telling me this because we

are?" Natalie's voice was raised.

"No, but your support would be nice. It's hard on Dad."

"He's the one who wanted the job!" she yelled.

"Natalie Lee!" Now, Susan was yelling, too. "You are so rude and self-centered!"

"And I thought we were getting along."

"I thought so, too."

They were at a standstill. There was nothing more that needed to be said. Susan went to the kitchen and Natalie to her room.

Susan called Maryann, planning to invite herself to tea. Maryann gladly allowed Susan to invite herself over.

Fluffy jumped at Susan when she came through Maryann's door. "She doesn't like me."

"Sure she does," Maryann laughed.

"It isn't funny," Susan sounded serious. "Can you put her in your room?"

"Of, course, if you're afraid."

"I am," admitted Susan. "I don't like yippy little dogs attacking me."

"Come on, Fluffy, I'll put you away. You're scaring Susan."

Susan glanced around Maryann's immaculate house. Every pillow on the couch was angled perfectly; there wasn't a hint of dust anywhere, or clutter. She spied the photograph of that woman on Maryann's desktop. As she picked it up, Maryann came into the room.

"The coast is clear, attack dog is confined." Maryann saw Susan handling the photograph.

"You aren't going to ask me about that again, are you? I told you I put it out so I'd have a photo on display like everyone else."

"Tell me about this old friend," Susan pursued it.

"Oh all right, let me fix some tea."

Maryann served almond tea and ginger cookies on a rose wood engraved tray. She had flowered napkins, too.

Maryann touched her hair, and swallowed noticeably before talking. She told Susan about the days when she would walk to high school with this person, share lockers, sweaters, and secrets together. Her face was blank, devoid of emotion while talking.

Susan was used to Maryann being lively while talking and smiling a lot. She wondered if the friend had died tragically or fallen to misfortune. It seemed that there was something sad and almost unfinished about her story.

"Is this woman alive?" Susan asked.

"I don't know. I haven't seen her for twenty years."

"Couldn't you look her up somehow?" Susan suggested.

"Maybe I could help. I'm home. Give me some information, her name, her…"

Maryann cut Susan off, "Forget about it. I knew her in high school. Let it go. It's just a photo."

Susan decided not to push it. But she was definitely interested in pursuing it again, someday.

"Fine. What do you want to talk about?"

Maryann showed Susan the wicker chair she'd purchased at an auction the day before. They'd always gone to auctions and garage sales before Jeff started working out of town. Susan missed it, but missed Jeff more.

"That's gorgeous."

"Thanks." Maryann then asked Susan when it was a good time to try a home pregnancy test.

Susan's eyes opened as wide as possible. "A pregnancy

test?"

"Yes, Susan. I had sex with Gordon. Unprotected sex."

"Why?"

"Why? You know why. I want to have a baby."

"I know, but I imagined the two of you marrying one day and having a family. Not this wham, bam, thank you ma'am stuff for you. My goodness Maryann. What were you thinking?"

"For once I wasn't thinking. I was listening to my heart. I want a baby. I need a man to give me that. So I had a man."

"I don't know about you." Susan sipped her tea, and munched on a cookie. She wondered if she ever really knew her friend at all.

Maryann changed the subject to something less controversial and light.

Chapter 8

Natalie and Johnny had intercourse again. This time Natalie didn't hate it, but didn't like it, either. She wanted to tell someone, but was afraid. She knew the risks, but her need to keep Johnny had won out. He'd been distant and uninterested. So she'd suggested they "do it" again.

And then the problem began.

"Mom, do you ever have female problems?"

"What do you mean?"

Natalie described her problem.

"You'd better go to the doctor," Susan said. She wanted Jeff there so badly. She wished it were Wednesday. Again, she thought about moving. "Maybe we should."

But in the meantime, she needed to help her daughter. Susan wasn't sure what was wrong with Natalie, but she suspected her daughter might have contracted a sexually transmitted disease. She bit her tongue, before saying something that would alienate her daughter. "Let's see what the doctor says," she thought. "Then the talking will have to happen."

Judy slipped into her body suit and slacks. She felt pretty and youthful sleeping with Johnny, but she knew they had to be careful. If Beetle knew, he'd hate her. And she loved her son. She stroked her hair with a rattail comb, and smiled at her reflection in the mirror.

"You going to Mr. Swanson's?" she asked her son. She hoped he was.

"Yeah, why? You got a hot date?"

"Maybe."

"Good for you, Ma."

Judy tousled her son's hair playfully.

"Hey, have a good time. It must be nice for you to be around a man, you not having a father around."

"It is, Ma."

"I don't think Swanson and I are going to get together, but that's okay. As long as you can spend time together."

"See ya."

"Stay out as late as you want. Hell, sleep over if he asks ya."

Beetle thought it was weird to think about sleeping over at an old teacher's house, but why not? They were more like buddies now, anyway. "Okay," he said.

As soon as he left, Judy called Johnny. He agreed to come over. She was more than ready for him.

The doctor's visit was a strain. Natalie had protested, but her worry over what was wrong with her overshadowed her protests.

This was her first time being examined by a gynecologist. She hated it. As Susan suspected, the doctor told her she had a disease that is transmitted sexually. Natalie had the choice to tell or not tell her mother and she decided to tell her. Natalie cried. Susan felt a number of emotions, but kept calm for Natalie's sake. They left in silence.

When they arrived home, Natalie spoke. "I'm sorry, Mom. I'm never going to have sex again. Ever!"

"Natalie, it isn't sex that is wrong or bad. It is having sex when you aren't ready, or the time isn't right. I hate to say it, but Johnny must be having sex with others, too."

"I don't want to talk about that."

"I know you don't, but you should. Your father and I have a wonderful sex life, one we've worked at for years."

"Mom," her voice sent the message that she didn't want to hear about her parents' sex life.

"You will have that some day, too. I know you will. What you have can be cleared up with medicine, and not having sex with Johnny."

She'd embarrassed her daughter by saying that, but didn't care. "You are fortunate that you didn't contract something worse, although we won't know about the AIDS test until that comes back, but at least you're not pregnant." Then Susan sensed it was a good time to back off, and give Natalie a chance to take it all in.

"Do you mind if I call Johnny. I want to tell him off." "I don't mind."

Natalie went to her room, but her call was incomplete, as he wasn't home. She cried herself to sleep, instead.

What Beetle saw in his mother's room shocked him. He'd returned home to get a few things so he could spend the night at Mr. Swanson's. Gordon had been delighted with the idea.

It didn't bother Beetle that he could hear his mother having sex, he'd heard it before. It was the sight of Johnny's backside on top of her as he'd passed by the open door to get to his room that bothered him.

He kept his feelings in. He didn't tell them he was home, or confront them. He packed more than one night's worth, though. He was going to see if he could move in with Swanson. He didn't want to live there anymore. A tear moved down his cheek as he walked out the door.

Jeff entered the office in time to see his secretary bending over her desk attending to something.

"Jeff, I've lost a contact." She continued in her bent over position to closely examine the top of her desk. "Oop, there it is."

She proceeded to stick it back on her eye. "All set."

Jeff felt sweaty, nervous. The sight of her bent over did things to him he wasn't proud of as a happily married man.

"Oh, did I tell you?" he spoke jerkily. "My wife is coming up Wednesday."

"That's nice," she said. "But if you ever want me to, I'd be happy to keep you company."

"What?"

"Well, you know, because you're here all alone."

"Oh, well, thanks, but I'm fine." Jeff had to admit he felt flattered to think that this woman wanted to spend time with him, but he had a feeling that she was thinking of more than just hanging out talking about school stuff together.

Susan got teary eyed seeing Jeff Wednesday night. She was closer to thinking of moving than she'd ever imagined she'd be, and now that Natalie wasn't interested in Johnny, it might be easier for her to think about it, too, Susan thought.

"Why don't you start looking for houses, Jeff."

"Are you serious?" He was overjoyed, but surprised by her suggestion. "You'd consider selling our house and moving?"

"I guess I would, I want to be together all the time again."

Jeff felt relieved, because he'd felt guilty about being tempted by his secretary and was "in love" with his wife all over again. "You are amazing."

"I know, and you're lucky I'm yours," she said.

"I know that, too."

They enjoyed a Chinese all-you-can-eat buffet, talked

about Natalie, laughed and joked and felt sad when it was time for Susan to leave.

"I'll start looking for houses tomorrow." Jeff looked sad for a moment.

"What's wrong?" asked Susan.

"Nothing," answered Jeff. "I'm really happy."

"I'm happy, too."

Susan drove home thinking about moving. The hardest part for her about the move was to leave her friend Maryann.

Susan picked up a lead in locating the woman in the photo in Maryann's house. She was determined to find her, especially now with thoughts of moving away. Susan went to the high school Maryann graduated from and asked to look at a yearbook. She flipped through until she found the photo. The woman's name was Jill. Susan asked if she could photocopy the page in the yearbook. The secretary made her a copy.

Susan was thrilled. She'd wanted to do this for Maryann as a kind of going away present. Next, she called a number she had for a private investigator. She was pumped up. It was a change from her daily routine. It was exciting.

"I'll see what I can do," said the investigator, after Susan gave him the information she had.

"Thanks," said Susan. She got home in time to watch the BOLD AND THE BEAUTIFUL.

During first period Natalie told Johnny that she didn't want to see him anymore. He didn't even pretend to appear sad. "You asshole," she said as she ran off to her next class.

Beetle avoided Johnny. He kept his feelings in. Judy wasn't saddened by her son's desire to move out, after all. She wished him well. She was obsessed with her young lover. And Gordon was overjoyed with the new arrangement.

Gordon was surprised by a call from Maryann. He

didn't think he needed her since he'd stolen her keys and slipped in to the lab late at night to photograph bones.

"Well, this is a surprise," he commented.

Maryann had failed the home pregnancy test and swallowed any pride she had left to call him to try to get him to come over to her place again.

"Would you still like the tour of the lab?" she asked.

"Tour?" He played dumb. "Oh sure." He figured, why not? Maybe she could give him some bones. It might be worth it, he thought. They planned to get together that Friday evening.

"Hey Beetle," Natalie called out in the school corridor.

"Hey, Natalie," Beetle sounded depressed. The neat guy stuff at Swanson's was fun, but he missed his mother and Johnny.

"Are you okay?" Natalie felt generous with her time these days. She'd barely given Beetle the time of day, but with Johnny out of the picture she needed friends.

"Yeah."

"I know this sounds funny coming from me and all, but my mom is making me go to this church thing this weekend, and I was wondering if you might like to go, too?"

Beetle couldn't believe what he was hearing. Natalie was asking him to sort of spend the weekend with her. He answered quickly before she could change her mind. "Heck sure, why not."

"Oh, great!" Natalie wanted to be close to someone who was close to Johnny. She hated Johnny, and then again she didn't. "Stop by my house after school for the details."

"You bet," Beetle was happy. He'd had a crush on Natalie forever.

Gordon went along with Beetle's weekend plan. He had the tour with Maryann, anyway. "Does your mother know?"

"Ah, who cares about her."

Gordon knew that was what he needed to hear to keep his young friend. A weekend away wouldn't hurt anything.

Chapter 9

The private investigator was amazing. He had an address for Jill after only one day. Susan left right away.

The ride was pleasant. Susan occupied herself with thoughts of meeting the woman, getting her together with Maryann, moving and being with Jeff full time, and Natalie breaking up with Johnny and not having sex until she is more ready for it. She felt great.

The houses were tract style. Susan found the right address easily. The woman even answered the door.

"Hello," said Susan. "I am a friend of an old friend of yours. Would it be all right if I talk to you about her?" Susan looked at the woman, who had pretty eyes, was modestly dressed, and had a small child saddled to her hip.

"Who's the old friend?" she asked.

"Maryann."

Jill glanced at the child, then over Susan's head, then focused on Susan's face. "Did she send you?"

"No," Susan answered. "I came on my own."

"Come in." Susan followed her through a clutter toy strewn house to what looked like a family room. "Just shove the junk onto the floor and sit down," Jill instructed. "Would you like coffee or tea?"

"A cup of tea, please."

Susan made small talk with the child while Jill made tea. Susan noticed a shelf with photos on it, and saw Maryann's senior picture among them. It was eerie. Why hadn't these two kept in touch, Susan wondered?

"Would you like milk or sugar?"

"No thanks."

"I like mine with lots of sugar and enough milk to make it look muddy," Jill said.

Susan noted that that was a different way to describe it. "I suppose you wonder why I'm here," Susan started.

"Well, yes," Jill said. "I suppose you are Maryann's lover."

Shock waved over Susan's entire body. She couldn't breathe, let alone speak. How could this woman suggest such a scenario, she wondered.

"I'm sorry," Jill said. "I assumed, since Maryann and I were lovers in high school, that that's how you know her."

Susan set her tea down. She wanted to get out of there. She felt nauseous.

"Relax," said Jill. "I just assumed you knew."

"No," Susan responded in a weak voice. "I'm her neighbor," she paused. "I thought," she paused again, "her friend, although it's obvious I don't know her at all."

Jill smiled thoughtfully. "Don't be too hard on her. We have to keep quiet about being lesbians. It isn't easy."

"But you have a home and a child," Susan appeared confused.

"Yes," Jill explained, "I'm living with a woman who is divorced and this is her daughter."

Susan was so uncomfortable; she got up to leave. "I'd better go, I'm sorry I bothered you."

"But I want to hear about Maryann. You see she broke up with me. Said something about our love being a sin to God. Or something like that."

Susan didn't know what to do next. "Would you like

her phone number?"

"Sure, but I'll have to hide it from my roommate. She's pretty jealous."

Susan felt nauseous again, hearing Jill say what she'd said. She wrote the number down, handed it to Jill, and left.

The ride home was a blur. She had a million thoughts crowding her head. She was surprised she'd made it home without getting into an accident, she felt so disoriented. Susan considered herself an open-minded person, but Maryann "a lesbian?" The idea made her ill. Every hug they'd shared now became suspect. "Oh, that's silly," Susan scolded herself. "She's still my best friend."

At home she put her feet up and flicked on the last fifteen minutes of AS THE WORLD TURNS.

"Mom, can my friend Beetle go with me this weekend?" Natalie asked Susan.

"I don't see why not. They always want more young people."

Natalie entered the family room with Beetle.

"Hey," he greeted.

"Hello, Beetle, how are you?" Susan asked.

"Not bad."

Natalie chimed in with, "Did you know that Beetle is living with Mr. Swanson?"

"Really?"

"My ma and me were having problems, so I moved in with Mr. Swanson."

"Oh," Susan wasn't sure how to react. "That's too bad."

"It's okay," he said, "Swanson's cool. I don't have a real father thing goin' in my life, so maybe it's for the best."

"Can we have chips, Mom?" Natalie played hostess.

"Yeah, help yourselves. There is COKE in the fridge."

Natalie and Beetle went to the kitchen for snacks and hung out until Beetle was going to leave.

"Isn't he a sweetheart?" Natalie asked her mother after Beetle left.

"Seems nice." Susan was used to Natalie's ever changing attitudes towards her peers. They were either awesome, or cool, a sweetheart or a dork.

"We are going to have so much fun!"

Of course, Susan was hoping Natalie would hang around the twins, but Natalie had always been more comfortable around boys than girls. I'm not going to obsess about this; at least we've been getting along lately, Susan thought.

"Natalie, I told your father to start looking at houses." Susan dared to bring up the "moving" subject to her daughter.

"You did?"

"Yes, I'm tired of not being together all the time."

"Fine."

"You mean it?"

"I just don't want to talk about it. If we move, we move." Natalie almost welcomed it after breaking up with Johnny.

"You are a pretty neat kid," Susan said to Natalie. You just never know, she thought.

"Thanks."

"God doesn't make junk!" Natalie quoted their minister.

"Hey, maybe I'll come back from this weekend, a religious fanatic."

"That wouldn't be so bad, would it?"

Natalie laughed, "Yeah right, Mom."

It was fun for them both to be able to joke around.

The phone rang; it was Maryann wondering if Susan could go over. "I'm sorry, I'm busy with Natalie," Susan begged off.

Natalie looked at her mother like, "It's okay Mom, go." But Susan stuck to her excuse. She was afraid that Jill had contacted Maryann, and Maryann knew that she knew about Jill, now.

"I can see her another time," said Susan. "I want to hang out with you, if that's all right."

"Sure Mom, that's cool." They watched Natalie's favorite TV shows, shared a bowl of popcorn and frozen heated up pizza.

Maryann was delighted that Susan and Natalie were getting along. She'd called to ask Susan over, so she could get some advice about her relationship with Gordon. Wanting to try for some traditional values in her life she thought, "Maybe we could get married someday and have the baby together." Then her phone rang.

"Hello."

"It's Jill, Maryann."

Maryann dropped the phone to her chest. The sound of Jill's voice was almost too much for her.

"Are you there?" Jill asked.

"I am."

"So, how are you?"

"Fine, Jill."

"Is something wrong? I just wanted to hear your voice again and see if you are okay."

"I'm sorry, I don't know what to say."

"Do you have anyone in your life?"

"I'm seeing a man, a Science teacher."

"Oh, I see," Jill responded. "I'm living with a woman

who has a little girl. We're very happy."

"Oh, that's nice."

"Can I call again?"

"Maybe you shouldn't. It's been so long."

"Very well, Maryann. Have a good life." Click.

Maryann hung the phone up after several moments passed. Tears flooded her face. All the feelings of her youth returned. The memories were vivid, disturbing. "I thought I was over all this." Fluffy yipped at her to stop crying, but she couldn't.

Chapter 10

Natalie and Beetle sat together at dinner. They were served ham slices, home fries, green beans and applesauce. An energetic young man led a rousing rally of "Hallelujah. Let me hear it. Hallelujah. Amen."

At first Natalie and Beetle mocked it, but by the end of the rally they were into it.

After listening to several speakers, and hymn singing, they broke up to find their rooms. Beetle felt great walking with Natalie. He loved her wavy hair and bratty manner. He was crushed when she wanted to talk about Johnny.

"Your wonderful Johnny," he said, "is having sex with my mother! That's why I moved out!" Natalie slapped his arm hard.

"Shut up!" She couldn't believe it.

"It's true Nat," Beetle said. "I wish it wasn't."

Natalie looked on the verge of tearing up. Beetle invited her to his room. They were allowed to visit each other's rooms until bedtime, as long as they left their doors open.

They sat on Beetle's bed and Beetle chatted away. Natalie felt numb, so she barely responded. When Natalie had had enough, she got up to leave. "Thanks, Beetle," she said. "You are a good friend." She leaned in to give him a hug. "I hate Johnny," she said softly.

"I know, I do, too," he agreed, clinging to her for a moment before letting go.

"Don't forget to say your prayers." Natalie smiled.

"You, too."

Maryann tried to act interested in Gordon, but the call from Jill kept nagging at her.

"Are you feeling okay, Maryann?" Gordon had noticed that something was bothering her. "Do you want to lie down?" Gordon thought she might want to have sex again.

Maryann figured he wanted to have sex again. She was depressed and thought again that maybe she should work harder at this relationship. "Maybe I could be happy if I really tried," she whispered.

They went to the bedroom and had a repeat of the first time. Gordon whispered, "Shall we have that tour, now?"

"Now?" she couldn't believe it.

"Yeah, now." He waited for her to say something, but she didn't. "You sort of promised."

Maryann felt shame, embarrassment, and humiliation.

"Fine," she mumbled. In her heart she knew she couldn't keep doing this. They dressed without looking at each other, and then they drove separately to her lab.

Gordon asked for some discarded bones, which she gave to him, thinking they were for his class, and allowed him to take pictures, although she found it strange that he'd brought a camera.

When they walked to their cars, she knew it would be for the last time. I can't do this again, she thought.

"Can we do this again?" he asked.

"I don't think so," she answered. "I'm going to be quite busy the next few weeks."

"Oh well, it's been fun." Actually Gordon didn't care. He had what he'd wanted. He didn't need to see her anymore, either.

Chapter 11

Susan answered her phone with just woken up voice.

"Can you come down to the station?" a voice asked her.

"Who is this?"

"It's Maryann."

"What station…train?"

"Police."

"What is going on?"

"I'll tell you when you get here."

Susan was dumbfounded. What would Maryann be doing at the Police Station, she wondered?

It was Monday morning. Natalie had come back from her weekend, acting like a new person. She was enthusiastic, and ready to start fresh at school. Susan was encouraged to see such a positive change in her daughter.

Susan had enjoyed her weekend with Jeff all to herself. They hadn't wasted a moment on negative thoughts or problems.

Susan dressed quickly and left, telling Natalie that Maryann needed to see her, without going into where.

Detective Wallace greeted her at the front desk, and showed her to the room Maryann occupied. Maryann's face appeared frozen in fear, which made Susan even more nervous.

"Can someone please tell me what is going on?" Susan asked.

Detective Wallace stood six feet tall, was handsome and very professional acting.

"It seems that your friend was a bit careless," he said as he looked at Susan.

"Maryann? Careless?"

Maryann looked ill at this point. Susan felt sorry for her.

"It appears that your friend allowed a friend of hers to take photographs in the lab she works at."

Susan still wasn't sure what was going on. "What is this about?"

Wallace put a hand on his hip and used the other to point a finger at the two ladies. "This is quite serious."

Maryann looked guilty, now.

"Is this true?" Wallace asked Maryann.

"Maybe I should have a lawyer," Maryann said.

"At this point, no," he answered.

Maryann looked at Susan, then back to the detective.

"Am I being charged with something?"

"This is the deal," Wallace said. "What I am about to tell you has got to be kept quiet. It is strictly confidential. Do I have your word, ladies, that you will not discuss what I am about to tell you with anyone? Not even amongst yourselves?"

Susan swallowed hard and looked at her friend. What could this be? A mixture of emotions raced through her. This sure is a change from my everyday routine, she thought.

Maryann answered first, "I won't tell."

"I won't either," Susan agreed.

"Good," said Wallace, "because this is more serious than any photographs of bones." He took a deep breath before continuing. "This involves child pornography."

Maryann and Susan were in shock.

"Mr. Swanson is involved in the trafficking of pornographic materials involving children. We have been investigating him for the past year."

The two of them were stunned, numb, speechless, and totally disgusted.

Maryann spoke first, "What would you like me to do? I mean, how can I help?"

Susan felt proud of her friend.

"I want you to continue to see him."

"But," Maryann said, "I already told him I wouldn't be."

"Well, you'll have to change that. We need you to get into his house and attempt to locate his stash."

"What do you mean?"

"Child pornographers have photos and videos of children engaged in sexual activities. It is what they use for their own pleasure, as well as to sell to other sickos like themselves."

"Are you sure about this?" Susan didn't want to believe it. "Mr. Swanson has quite a wonderful reputation in the community. My daughter just spent the weekend with a young man who is living with him."

Wallace shook his head. "That's where we need your help. We know about Beetle living there. We want you to call us if he says anything strange about Swanson to you, anything at all."

"I barely know the kid."

"Maybe you could invite him over for dinner."

"And if we refuse?" Susan asked.

"I hate to use this, but Maryann was wrong to allow Swanson to photograph bones at the lab. We'll ignore that, if you ladies cooperate."

"I can understand involving me, but why Susan?"

"Because of her daughter's friendship with Beetle," he answered. "Well, ladies," he studied their faces. "Will you help us?"

They checked each other out, then nodded in agreement.

"I can't believe it," said Susan.

"I can't either," agreed Maryann. "Who would have ever suspected him?"

"Now that I think about it, Jeff always felt there was something not quite right about the guy."

Detective Wallace spoke up, "Most child pornographers are usually someone the community wouldn't suspect. They are often very intelligent, and described as people who care deeply about children. Feel free to discuss this here, but like I said, don't talk about this to anyone, not even each other, once you leave this room."

They both assured him that they wouldn't, even though Susan knew it would be difficult to keep from Jeff. They shared everything. On the other hand, it made it easier to avoid Maryann, now that she knew about her and her old friend Jill.

The halls were filled with friends chatting about the weekend that passed. Beetle waited at Natalie's locker. He loved every minute he'd spent with her at their retreat. He felt like he was in heaven, then Johnny appeared and he felt like he was in hell. His hatred reared its ugly head.

"Get lost, Johnny!"

"What?"

"You heard me, get out of here." Beetle was over the shock of seeing him with his mother, and was just angry, "I know about you and my ma."

Johnny stood there. "I'm sorry, man."

"Yeah right!"

"Where's Natalie?"

"I told you to get out of here. She doesn't want to see

you. I told her, you know."

"Are you serious?"

Beetle gave Johnny the most hateful look he was capable of giving anyone. Johnny started to walk away. Natalie appeared. Beetle hated to see them even near one another.

"Nat, I'm really sorry. I want to talk to you about all this." Johnny moved towards her.

Natalie slapped him hard across the face. "Don't come near me." Beetle cheered inside. He'd wanted her to do that. Johnny held his cheek.

"You're such a bitch!" said Johnny. "And don't come around me, anymore, Beetle."

"As if!" Beetle responded. Natalie and Beetle shared a brief moment after Johnny left. She felt good. She'd felt a lot of good feelings after the weekend. She especially felt like smiling more, too.

Maryann didn't have to invent an excuse to see Gordon again; she'd passed her second home pregnancy test. She was going to have his baby. The thought sickened her after learning what he was about.

She phoned him. "Gordon, I need to see you."

"But I thought you were busy."

"I'm pregnant."

"You are?"

"Yes. Can we get together? I was hoping I could come to your place this time?"

"My place?" he said. "Well, okay."

They planned it out for Thursday.

Gordon hung up the phone. He was mad. "This isn't good," he thought. This kind of thing was all new to him. He asked Beetle if he could go somewhere that Thursday.

"Don't worry, Swanson. I'll see about going to

Natalie's."

Susan drove the speed limit plus five. She was eager to meet Jeff for dinner again. The weekend had been so wonderful, having the house to themselves. She knew it would be difficult to not tell about the Swanson business, but she'd given her word.

They met at a seafood place. The tables were very private.

Susan held Jeff's hands tightly across the table.

"I found a great house," he said.

"A what?"

"A three bedroom house."

"Oh." She was happy, but preoccupied with so much on her mind.

"What's the matter?" Jeff asked. "I thought that's what you wanted."

"It is, don't worry about me. I'm expecting my period." She again shoved back the desire to tell him about Swanson and then there was the Maryann, lesbian thing.

"Are you going to have time to go back to my room before you head back home tonight?"

Susan squeezed his hands. "You bet I will. You don't think I came all this way to 'eat and run,' do you?" They laughed, just as the waitress brought their dinners. They'd ordered shrimp Creole and fluffy white rice. Jeff said the blessing. "Dear Lord, help us find the way to be together as a family all the time. The way we should be. Amen."

Jeff was eager for them to move there. His secretary was getting to him more each day. He even thought of letting her go, but wasn't sure if that was right. What would he say, "I need to let you go, because you are tempting me?" He was ashamed of his feelings.

"Do you know how lonely I am here by myself?" Jeff said.

"I'm lonely, too."

"But you have familiar surroundings, and Natalie, speaking of, how is she? This is the first time you haven't complained about something she's said or done. What's going on?"

"I have nothing to complain about. We're getting along great." Susan shared briefly about the good weekend she had at her retreat and her break up with Johnny, sparing him the details.

"Sounds like a good time to move," said Jeff.

"Yeah," Susan felt the same, except for wanting to help with the investigation and have a heart to heart with Maryann, if she could figure out what she'd say to her, that is.

But once back to Jeff's room, she emptied her head of all of that and gave her entire being to the act of making love to her husband.

She took her time and kissed him slowly. It was like a studied art form. She was sculpturing his tongue with her own. The warm wetness excited their bodies, and a fine sweat covered them both as they put into practice the techniques they'd discovered through the years.

She breathed in short breaths as he kissed the most sensitive areas on her body. She wanted to enter his body and stay there. Wanted to breathe his breath and share his heartbeats. Her mouth found his most sensitive areas, too. And then their bodies became one.

Later while they snuggled, Susan said, "Buy that house. I don't care what it looks like. I need to be with you every day."

"You mean it, Suze?"

"You bet I do."

They made a plan for Susan to bring Natalie up that weekend, instead of Jeff going home. They planned to show her around, and let her get used to the idea.

"You're not bad for an old lady," Jeff teased as Susan got into her car to go back.

"You'll never have better," she reminded him.

"You got that right." He kissed her long, to last until Friday night.

"Miss you already."

"Miss you, too."

Jeff knew he'd never have better, but his lustful feelings for his secretary were definitely out of control. He knew he had to do something about it. He would never purposely hurt Susan. He knew she did not deserve to be married to a cheater.

Chapter 12

Susan wasn't prepared for Natalie's reaction to the weekend trip to see the house.

"I don't want to," she said. "I know I said I would, but I can't. I want to live here. Please don't make me." She ran off to her room crying.

"Oh Lord, what now?" Susan went to the kitchen to put the teakettle on. The phone rang. It was Maryann. Susan felt awkward about getting together, but invited her over.

"What kind of tea do you want?" Susan asked predictably.

"Mint, if you have it. My stomach is a bit upset."

"Are you ill?"

"No, just pregnant."

"Really?" It was hard for Susan to get excited now, knowing about the baby's father.

"Can you believe it?" Maryann laughed her melodious laugh. Susan imagined Maryann sharing her laugh with Jill. She wondered if she'd shared that beautiful laugh with Gordon, probably not. Just get me pregnant, and get away, she thought. Susan wasn't proud of her thoughts, but she couldn't turn them off. She didn't want to hug Maryann anymore, either, now that she knew. It seemed too strange.

"Well, congratulations," she said.

"Thanks."

Susan couldn't bring herself to say more.

"I know it should be different, now, after you know,"

she trailed off, "but I'm so excited about having a baby, I can't think about anything else."

Susan couldn't fake it. She thought, "Maryann is a lesbian, and I never knew it. Now she is pregnant by a child pornographer. What am I supposed to say? How am I supposed to react?"

"Are you okay?" Maryann asked Susan. "I know that thing we can't talk about is upsetting."

"You are right. We can't talk about it." Susan poured the boiling water into their mugs. Her mug had SUSAN printed on it and Maryann's had a bunch of painted daisies.

"Sorry, I won't," said Maryann. "But are you sure you are all right?"

Susan cleared her throat before telling her the news. "We're going to move to Jeff's school district. It's what I want, but Natalie is having a hard time with it."

Maryann sat silent for a few moments, then said, "I had no idea you were even considering this," she paused. "I don't know what to say. I uh, wow, I'm really going to miss you. Would you like me to talk to Natalie? Would that help?"

"No!" Susan was quick to object. The lesbian business bothered her more than she'd realized. It was okay to think about people being gay when you heard about it on a talk show, but uncomfortable to think about in your best friend, she thought. She was ashamed of her feelings, but that was how she felt.

"Okay," Maryann said. "You need to do this yourself. I understand."

No you don't, thought Susan.

"It'll be hard for me," she said tipping her head down.

"I know," Susan agreed, wanting to touch her hand like she would have before she knew, but she refrained this time.

"As much as I hate to see you leave, I understand. Whatever I can do…" Maryann searched Susan's face for a response.

"I know."

They sipped their tea until Maryann made a move to leave. "Thanks for the tea."

"You're welcome. And congratulations on becoming a mother. It won't be easy, but I know you'll be a good one." No matter how confused and uncomfortable Susan was about Maryann's sexual preference, she believed Maryann would be a good mother.

Jeff walked into the office and planned to have a serious talk with his secretary about her questionable friendliness and offers of getting together. She sat at her desk. He noticed she had on an attractive v-neck top, which was very flattering to her large breasts and small waist. He knew this was not going to be easy.

"Can we talk?" he said.

"Oh, sure Boss, what's up?"

"I appreciate your friendliness and offers to get together," he was getting sweaty again and nervous, "but I don't want there to be any misunderstanding between us."

"Misunderstanding?" She looked at Jeff as if she didn't know what he was getting at.

Jeff was embarrassed. He knew he couldn't have read her wrong. He'd seen it before. Women coming on to men. Long thought to be the men who did the coming on, it wasn't so much that way anymore, he'd observed.

"Well, anyway, I thank you for the invitations, but I'm a happily married man and well," he wanted out of the conversation.

"Oh," she giggled. "I understand. But if you change

your mind, I'm available." She turned back to her work as if she was just talking business.

Jeff went to his office, more disturbed than ever. He'd set out to send a message and may have made the problem worse, he thought. He hoped Susan and Natalie moved quickly. He was ashamed of what this attractive "available" woman was doing to him.

As much as Susan dreaded it, she had to talk to Natalie. She was spoiled with a few good times with her. Ups and downs, that's all it is. One day you're up, the next day you're down, she thought.

"Nat, can we talk?" she knocked at her door.

A groan came from within.

"Can we?"

"Yes!" she yelled. Susan entered the room. There was a pile of clothes on the floor about two feet high. Susan could feel nagging words rising up in her throat, but let them stick there. She had more important things to talk to Natalie about.

"I thought we'd talked about moving and you were okay with it."

"I thought I was," said Natalie.

"What changed that?"

"Promise you won't get mad?" Natalie gave a quick glance at her mother, then looked down again.

"Why would I get mad?"

"Trust me, Mom, you will when you hear it."

Out of curiosity, Susan promised she wouldn't.

"Johnny was here when you met Dad."

"What?" Susan blew up.

"I told you you'd get mad."

"What were you thinking? I thought you two broke up." Susan sounded distraught. "And you know how I feel about boys over when no one is home, especially now that you two have…"

"Mom! Listen to me! Nothing happened. I wouldn't do that. I wouldn't do that here. We just talked. He begged me to listen. He was really sweet. I had to give him that."

"But Nat," Susan shook her head back and forth, not wanting Johnny within ten feet of her daughter, "don't tell me you're back together?"

"Yes and no."

"What is that supposed to mean?"

"We are, but no more sex."

"Oh Lord, Natalie, grow up!"

"Please leave my room, Mom!" Natalie was crying and screaming like she always did when she couldn't handle something. "You're always putting me down. I hate it. I thought things were different."

"So did I." Susan left the room. She was too upset, and disappointed, and tired. "Natalie seemed so different after being away last weekend," Susan mumbled under her breath.

"Lord, I need help," she prayed. All the way down the steps she summoned the Lord. She wanted an answer to her prayer for help with Natalie. She believed the move was an answer to prayer. But would it be enough, she wondered. "Lord, please hear my prayer."

Thursday night Beetle showed up at the house. Susan was surprised.

"I can't believe Natalie went back to that jerk," he said.

"Especially after what I told her," he shook his head.

"What did you tell her," Susan asked.

"That he was sleeping with my mother."

"You've got to be kidding."

"No, I'm not. That's why I moved in with Swanson."

The sound of that name made Susan shiver. If she couldn't save her own daughter from making a big mistake, she figured she might be able to save Beetle.

"Move back home!" Susan commanded.

"What?" he looked confused.

"Move back home." She had to make him do it. He was better off with a mother who sleeps with teens than a child pornographer. Not much, but better.

"No way, I hate her."

"But she's your mother."

"I don't care."

Susan wasn't getting anywhere trying to get him to move home so she tried something else. "Move in here."

"In here?"

"Yes, at least until we move."

"You guys are moving?" Beetle was not thrilled with the news.

"We want to be near Nat's Dad. Now we only get to see him on weekends."

"Oh."

Susan asked him to stay for dinner and they could talk more about it. He went to the family room to watch TV until dinner.

When Natalie and Johnny walked in Susan immediately tensed up, and it was obvious.

Johnny was holding Natalie around the waist. Susan held back the temptation to say, "Get your hands off my daughter."

"Hi, Mom," Natalie's voice was cool. "Johnny's here."

"I see."

"I'd better go," Johnny said.

Susan didn't say anything.

"Okay," Natalie said.

"Good bye." He looked at Susan.

Susan remained silent. She didn't care if the kid was good looking. She just kept picturing him on top of Natalie and now on top of Beetle's mother. The images made her sick.

"You could have been friendly, Mom."

"Why should I?"

"Because of me."

"Well, I think you're being stupid."

"Oh, so now I'm being stupid? Thanks a lot!"

"Keep your voice down. Beetle's in the family room."

"What's he doing here?"

"He was looking for a friend. I invited him for dinner."

"Oh great!" Natalie said. "But you couldn't invite Johnny?"

"No."

"Fine."

"Fine, yourself." They sounded like two-year-olds.

"Now, go talk to Beetle."

"Okay!" Natalie stormed off.

Beetle was watching MTV when Natalie joined him.

"Hey, Beetle."

"Hey," he said, not looking away from the TV. He was disgusted with her.

"What are you doin'?"

"Just hangin' out. Your mom asked me to stay for dinner."

"I know, I suppose you heard about me and Johnny."

"Yeah."

"What do you think about it?"

"What am I supposed to think?"

"Isn't he your best friend?"

103

"Was, until he slept with my ma." He turned away from the TV and looked at Natalie. "I had a great time with you last weekend. I never went to church stuff before. You got a great house, nice Mom, cool Dad, and you want to go out with a jerk! I don't get it, Natalie!"

"Don't talk like that about Johnny!"

"I gotta go," Beetle hopped out of the chair. "Tell your Mom thanks anyway."

Natalie was confused. She knew she wasn't sure about Johnny, but she'd loved him for a long time. She plopped down on the couch and switched the channel to the soap opera she watched after school, THE GUIDING LIGHT.

"Natalie, time for dinner," Susan said. "Where's Beetle?"

"He said he had to go, and wanted me to tell you thanks anyway."

They ate without talking. It was strained, until Natalie broke the silence.

"Go ahead, Mom. Say whatever you want to. You've already said I'm stupid," then the tears. "Doesn't anyone remember what it's like to be in love?"

"Natalie, there is love, and there is lust. You may love Johnny, but it seems that he is in lust, and not with just you."

"Oh, Mom!" Natalie yelled, as if her mother couldn't hear her, as if she could never in her lifetime understand.

"Natalie, your father and I are in love. We've spent the last twenty-five years trying to make each other happy."

"Don't talk about Dad."

"Why not?"

"I don't know, I guess I miss him so much."

Was that what this was all about, Susan wondered. Natalie had always been a handful, but so much worse since

Jeff had been away. Susan got up and hugged her daughter from behind.

Natalie resisted at first, then turned around in her seat to return the hug.

Sobbing, she said, "I'm sorry, Mom."

"I'm sorry, too." said Susan, also sobbing.

When they'd calmed down, Natalie told her mother that she missed her dad, but selfishly didn't want to move. Susan told her she would try to be more understanding.

They washed and dried the dishes together, something they hadn't done for awhile.

"Are you going to my track meet, Friday?"

"Sure, then after that we'll go to Dad's for the weekend to look the area over."

"Oh, okay," Natalie said. Her response was half-hearted, but at least she agreed, Susan thought.

Chapter 13

"Could you help me?" Jeff's secretary called from the filing room. He went to find her. School was over for the day and they were staying late to do reports. Everyone in the building was gone. She was reaching for a file on a high shelf and her top separated from her skirt, revealing bare skin.

Jeff felt aroused. He was completely humiliated that he felt this way. What is happening to me, he wondered. He knew he loved his wife, so why was he getting excited, seeing another woman's midriff?

When he was completely in the room she stopped reaching and shut the door behind him.

"What's going on?" he said.

"Don't you know?" She wrapped her arms around his waist and pushed her body up against his. "I've wanted you from the moment you started working here."

He knew the erection he felt would be obvious to her now that their bodies were so close. He was sweating his heartbeat was racing.

"You want me too, don't you?" she said in a husky sensual voice. He didn't answer. "Yeah I know you're married," she said, "but so what. We can have sex for fun, can't we? Nobody has to know, nobody but you and me."

It was incredible, he thought. Maybe she had a point. If it was just for fun, and if she didn't want anything else, what was the harm? Oh, Lord, what am I doing? I'll know he thought, and I'll never be able to tell Susan without it killing her and destroying what we have.

He pulled her arms away from around his waist, and said. "You're fired!"

"What?"

"You heard me, you're fired! Pack up your things and leave immediately!"

"You can't do that, I'll charge sexual harassment!" she said as she swiftly pulled off her top and her front hooked bra, revealing the breasts he'd only imagined to be so beautiful, and they were.

She pulled up her skirt, revealing that she had no panties on to which he pulled down his pants, revealing his erection. And they had sex, fast and hard. Jeff climaxed in no time.

Chapter 14

Maryann studied Gordon's rooms like she was studying for a final exam. She wished he would leave, so she could snoop. They had take-out Chinese food for dinner at the table in front of the TV. "Do you mind?" Gordon said, "I usually watch the news."

Maryann thought it was rude, but didn't object. After they were finished eating, she said, "Would you mind going out for peppermint ice cream? I'll pay for it. I'm having a craving." Maryann was proud of herself; she felt like a real detective, until he said, "I have that kind. That's my favorite, too. Isn't that neat?"

"Neat." Maryann would have to use another tactic to get him out of the house, so she could look for his stash.

While dishing up the ice cream, he said, "What about the baby?" but before she could say anything, he said, "I'm sorry, I'm not the marrying type. But I will certainly help out."

"Oh, don't worry," Maryann said. "I'm not the marrying type either. I just felt an obligation to tell you."

"Ha, what do you know. I guess we're okay with this, then, huh?"

"Yeah."

"Things change, don't they?" Gordon said. "If it were our parents' day, we'd be married, probably miserable, but we'd do it."

"Yup, probably miserable." Maryann felt miserable being in the same room with Gordon, now that she knew about his darker side.

Beetle burst into the room before they took their first bites of ice cream. "You gotta come with me!" he screamed at Gordon.

"Beetle, what is it?"

"I hurt my ma," he cried out. "I didn't mean it!"

"What are you talking about?"

"I'll tell you on the way over there."

Gordon looked at Maryann. "Do you mind?" he asked.

"No," I'll let myself out."

It was a gift, she thought. She couldn't have been more pleased. "I can snoop around, find what Detective Wallace wants me to find and never have to see the pervert again."

After she took a few bites of ice cream, she began. All the closets were okay, but there was one locked one. She poked around in Gordon's dresser, until she found a key that fit. Her stomach almost turned over when she started looking through its contents. Albums filled with young boys in sexual situations were stored on shelves, as well as videos; she could imagine how sick they were.

Leaving the house, she had thoughts of burning the place down, but figured he'd just move away and do the same things somewhere else. Once back home with Fluffy, she phoned Detective Wallace to report her findings.

"Good work, Maryann," the Detective praised her. He was ecstatic. After a year's worth of investigating he had what he needed to act make an arrest.

Chapter 15

Susan attended the track meet, but sporting events weren't her thing. Seeing young people transformed into hard, competitive beings disturbed her. And to top it off, she spotted Natalie and Johnny together, which made her angry. They waved to her.

"How can she trust that jerk?" Susan muttered.

In their jogging suits they looked innocent enough, but Susan knew better.

Young athletes were stretching out their bodies wherever she looked. She sat through event after event awaiting Natalie's turn. She was the last runner in her foursome for the 4X4 relay.

Susan stood, cheered for the girls, dutifully, and then Natalie grabbed the baton and off she went.

Natalie was heads ahead of everyone. She was pumped. She was a streak. Her ponytail flew behind her. People were yelling, "Go Natalie!" Susan was proud. She choked up.

When it was over, she rushed to the finish line to congratulate her daughter, who'd come in first. But Johnny got to Natalie before she could get there. Seeing them hug, made Susan angry again.

When they looked her way, Susan mouthed, "Congratulations," and motioned for Natalie to come over to her. Natalie appeared reluctant to leave Johnny's side, which further angered and embarrassed Susan.

When Natalie finally waltzed over to her mother, Susan hugged her and said, "Good job, Natalie."

Natalie was sweaty and fatigued. Susan thought she'd better remind her that they needed to leave, now that her event was over with. "We have to leave, Natalie."

"Oh, Mom, can't we stay awhile? I want to watch Johnny run."

"Your father is waiting for us."

"Oh fine!" she walked off towards the locker room. "But I still don't want to move!"

"Isn't parenting a joy!" Susan said aloud. Other parents heard, and some smiled and shook their heads.

The drive was painfully quiet. Susan had attempted to draw Natalie out with talk of the track meet, but Natalie was stubborn. She wouldn't warm up.

"If I'm less than thrilled about you and Johnny, it's only because I care about you."

Natalie finally looked at her mother, "I know, Mom." she gave a half-smile. Forced to keep her eyes on the road, Susan pretended that they had a great relationship. She kept up the fantasy, until she laid eyes on Jeff.

"You are a sight for sore eyes," he said. His corny greeting was welcome. Riding with the ice queen, Natalie, had not been enjoyable for Susan. "We won, Dad!" Natalie was cheery and enthusiastic for Jeff. Susan resented it, but was happy for them. They were in their own world for the next five minutes.

Then Jeff said, "Let me talk to Mom for a minute, then I'll take my girls out for dinner."

"I'll go to your room and watch TV." Natalie left.

Jeff was determined to never let Susan find out about his indiscretion. He was feeling painfully ashamed, and guilty. And it plagued him that he couldn't undo what he had done. He'd have to live with the knowledge that he'd committed adultery, for the rest of his life.

"Sweetheart," he said, "You'll never know how happy I am that you've decided to move here."

"Oh, I think I have a pretty good idea," Susan said. They hugged, and she did notice that he was squeezing her harder than usual. "Boy," she pulled away for a moment, "I guess you do miss me."

"Hmm, yup," he agreed. "I miss you more than I can say."

Their embrace turned into a desperate attempt for closeness, an almost starving person's need for sustenance.

Susan whispered, "Are you okay, dear?" Not that she wasn't feeling the same neediness, but she wondered if something was wrong.

Jeff welled up with tears, and buried his face in her shoulder.

"What is it?" she asked.

Between breaths and cries, that almost choked him, he said, "It's just that I love you so much, and would never want to lose what we have."

Susan held him, overjoyed that he was so enamored with her, and said, "Oh, sweetie, you are never going to lose me, don't be silly."

But Jeff wondered. If Susan ever did find out would she ever forgive his indiscretion? He wasn't strong enough right then to tell her, he knew he'd rather keep the ugly secret, than risk confessing and possibly lose her.

For different reasons, Susan felt about to cave in, too. The weight of her week was pressing in on her. She couldn't talk about the Swanson thing, didn't want to talk about the Maryann thing, and didn't feel like talking about the Natalie thing.

"Let's go eat," Jeff suggested.

"Good idea," Susan agreed.

They got Natalie and went to PIZZA HUT. It was obvious that Natalie looked bored with the whole thing. When she left for the restroom, Susan turned to Jeff and said, "Notice how miserable her highness is?"

"She's just unhappy about moving. She'll come around."

"I hope so."

When Natalie returned to the table Susan tried to get her to liven up. "Tell your dad about last weekend," she coaxed.

"Last weekend?" she looked totally blank.

"Last weekend with the youth group."

"Oh yeah, Mom loved having me gone." Natalie laughed. "Seriously, it was fun. I didn't think it would be, but it was."

"That's nice," said Jeff. "What kinds of things did you do?"

"We had great food, sang a lot of songs, attended church services, and oh, did you know Beetle went?"

"He did? How is Beetle?"

"Okay, I guess. He wasn't in school today, or at the track meet."

"He wasn't?" Susan expressed her concern. "Does he miss school a lot?"

"I don't remember him ever missing."

Jeff and Natalie chatted about the track meet again, while Susan worried about Beetle. She was determined to check on him as soon as she and Natalie returned home on Sunday.

Susan and Jeff loved the house Jeff had found. It was vacant, and they could move in any time.

Natalie made no comments about the house, but instead said, "Couldn't I live with Maryann, or something?"

Susan was not amused. "No you may not!"

"Gee Mom," Natalie said, "chill out."

Susan hated it when she said that.

"You'll like it here, Nat," said Jeff, the diplomat.

"Yeah right," complained Natalie under her breath, before getting into the car. It was time for Natalie and Susan to go back home.

"Do you really know how happy I am about this, Susan?" Jeff searched her face.

"I do," she said while hugging him tightly. "I'm happy, too."

Not long after they'd driven off, a terrible storm hit. Their car slid off the road. And they were stuck in the mud. Natalie screamed.

"Are you okay?" Susan screamed back.

"I don't know," groaned Natalie.

"Are you hurt?"

They weren't hurt; it was just awfully inconvenient being stuck in a ditch outside the town you'd just left. "When it lets up," Susan said. "We'll go find a house and use a phone.

"I can't believe this," Natalie said. "Stuck in the boonies. This sucks!"

"Natalie, you know I hate when you say that word."

"But doesn't it fit?"

Susan wouldn't agree out loud, but to herself she admitted that Natalie did have a point.

Susan put the radio on.

"Probably won't get any good stations," said Natalie.

"Oh, Natalie." Susan scanned until she found what she thought Natalie might like. "How is this?"

"It's okay."

They sat and listened until the rain let up. As Susan got out, Natalie scrambled to get out, too.

"You don't have to go," Susan said.

"Oh, yes I do," said Natalie. "I'm not staying in the car alone. A crazy person will probably try to get me."

"You are probably right." Susan rolled her eyes this time. "Come with me."

They trudged through puddles.

"I hate this," Natalie complained. "I want to go home."

"I thought you liked puddles," Susan teased.

"Very funny, Mom." Natalie managed a laugh, and splashed her mother in the puddle.

"Knock it off!" Susan yelled.

"Come on, Mom. I'm just trying to be fun. I suppose you are mad at me, now?"

"No Natalie, I'm not."

And then Susan jumped in a puddle, too.

Natalie was surprised. "So, you like puddles, now?"

"No, but I like you."

"Hmmm." Natalie put her arm around her mother's shoulders. Susan put her arm around her daughter's waist.

"Shall we walk to that farmhouse?" She pointed in the direction of a house down the road.

"Sure, Mom."

They hauled themselves out of the puddle, and were on their way.

The farmhouse was white with green trim. It looked well cared for. A young man, who looked about sixteen years old, answered the door. Susan could tell that Natalie was embarrassed to be seen wet and muddy. The young man was tall, blonde, and nice looking. He and Natalie made eye contact.

"Excuse us," Susan said. "Our car went off the road. Could we use your phone?"

"My phone?" He was staring at Natalie. "Well, I can help. I have a truck."

"We wouldn't want to impose."

"It's no problem," he responded. "I don't mind. Just stay here and I'll get my friends. We'll get the car out and bring it here." He left to get his truck out of the barn.

A woman with overalls on came into the room after he left. Susan explained to her what they were doing there.

The woman offered them the use of her bathroom to clean up, and a hot cup of tea.

After cleaning up as best they could, they sat around the kitchen table with their cups of tea.

"Does your son go to the Windrift School?" Natalie asked the woman.

"Yes, he does. The busses come out here to pick up the country kids."

"Hmmm."

Susan smiled. She knew right then that her daughter was going to be all right.

The car pulled out easily and was returned to the farmhouse. The young man's friends were obviously noticing Natalie, too.

"Don't forget to stop out," the woman said, "after you move here. We do a lot of fun things all year around."

Natalie smiled at the young man, who eagerly returned a smile.

Susan had offered to pay for the tow, but they would have no part of it.

"Thank you so much," she said. "Nice people," Susan commented as they drove away.

"Em huh," Natalie agreed.

"Thank you, Lord," Susan prayed silently. She felt warm, in spite of being chilled from the splashing, and thankful. What a lovely answer to prayer, she whispered.

Chapter 16

The house was dark when they arrived at home. Susan knew she'd miss the place, but the new place would be fine, too. At least they'd all be together, she thought.

Natalie headed for the shower. Susan checked the answering machine. There were two calls from Johnny. "Oh goody," she said sarcastically. There was one from Maryann and one from Beetle.

She daydreamed as she sat by the phone. Time passed, and before she realized it, Natalie was standing by her with clean wet hair and her warm robe on. "Your turn, Mom."

Susan welcomed the use of the bathtub, and planned to soak for awhile. Her daughter knocking on the bathroom door interrupted her soaking though.

"What is it?" Susan asked.

"Mom, Maryann is here," said Natalie from the other side of the bathroom door.

Susan jerked awake. She had dozed off; the water was cold, now. "Tell her I can't visit, um, I'll talk to her tomorrow."

Susan didn't feel like visiting. She wanted to dry off and go to bed.

The newspaper unfolded with the shocking news. Beetle's mother was dead. Beetle was being held under suspicion of causing her death.

"Natalie! Get down here!" Susan screamed. "I have something to tell you!"

"What the heck, Mom," Natalie bounded down the

stairs. "You sound like someone died."

"Someone did die," Susan tried to calm herself. "Look at the paper."

Natalie read the headlines. "Oh my God! He needs us!"

"Let's go." Susan was pleased with Natalie's show of compassion.

After they arrived at the police station, they were told that Beetle had been released to Mr. Swanson. The police had checked out Beetle's story and found that the death had been caused accidentally. It was true that mother and son had struggled and she fell, but swallowing a bottle of pills after Beetle had left caused her death.

"Mom, can we go to Mr. Swanson's?"

"I guess we'd better." The thought of Beetle at that man's house made Susan feel sick. And still, she had to pretend she knew nothing. After all, she'd promised the police.

"But you need to get to school, Natalie."

"I know Mom, please?"

Susan was thrilled again that her daughter was thinking about someone besides herself. "Okay, but then I'll bring you to school."

When they arrived, Beetle and Mr. Swanson were walking out of Swanson's front door.

"What are you doing here?" Beetle called out.

"We came to see how you're doing," Susan said. "We were just at the station."

"Oh." He put his head down.

"He's fine," said Mr. Swanson. "I'm taking him to school."

That did it! Susan was furious. She couldn't believe the lack of sensitivity Mr. Swanson was showing toward that kid he pretended to care about. "You can't go to school today!" she blurted out. "I'll take you to my house, we'll have lunch and talk."

"No," said Swanson. "I have to get to school, and he should, too."

"For God sakes! He just lost his mother, not to mention his being accused of causing her death!" She was livid.

"I know what I'm doing. I've handled kids who were grieving before." Swanson acted defensive.

"That may be true, but I've raised kids, so I know plenty. And I say the kid needs time." She was not about to let this pervert bully her or Beetle.

Beetle remained with his head down, like he could care less about anything.

"Come on, Beetle," Natalie called to him. Natalie's voice made the difference. He headed right towards their car.

"You are making a big mistake!" Swanson yelled at them. He appeared angry as they drove away.

Natalie said, "Mom, you were awesome." Susan could not have been more pleased. Maybe I finally impressed her, she thought, which made her smile.

They dropped Natalie off at school and drove to the church. It was Monday, and time to count the money. The secretary was friendly, as usual. She surprised Beetle by telling him that one of her twins had a crush on him. He forced a smile.

"Please come for dinner some evening soon," she said.

Beetle shook his head, seemingly pleased with the attention.

Susan made Beetle some grilled cheese sandwiches and tomato soup after they'd gotten home, something she'd always made for Max when he was home sick from school.

She asked him again if he'd like to stay with them until they moved.

"Well thanks," he said, "but Swanson's been good to me. I better stay there."

"No!" she almost gave it away. "I mean 'no problem.' I just wanted to help."

Susan excused herself and went to call Detective Wallace. She had to find out how the case was going. How much longer would Swanson the Creep be free, she wondered.

"The case is close to coming down," he said. "We need more time. We don't want to blow it."

"But this young man is hurting," said Susan. "And I'm afraid you-know-who will take advantage of that."

"I've told you all I can at this point," the Detective said.

"Fine," Susan returned, but she was not pleased. She did not want Beetle going back to Swanson's. She was going to try to figure out a way to keep him there.

"Would you stay tonight?" she asked Beetle. "You could sleep in Max's room."

"Well, okay," Beetle answered with a tone that communicated that he didn't care what he did.

"Good," Susan rejoiced inside. "I'll call Mr. Swanson at his school and let him know."

Susan left a message with the school secretary, after learning he'd taken his class outside.

"What is your favorite dinner?" Susan asked Beetle.

He answered with, "Why?" and a puzzled look on his face.

"Why?" his question caught her off guard. "I guess because I'd like to make you your favorite dinner."

"It doesn't matter."

"Yes it does," Susan insisted. "What is it?"

Beetle sighed, as if the thought of figuring out what his favorite dinner would be was a chore. Pizza and chips had been his mother's specialties. He'd usually fended for himself. He did recall a dinner he'd had years ago when she was having a boyfriend over.

"Can you make stuffed shells?"

"Yes I can. It's one of Natalie's favorite dinners, too."

"Thank you."

"It's my pleasure." Susan was excited. She thought about inviting Maryann over, too. She did feel guilty about avoiding her lately.

Maryann accepted over the phone. "Can I bring anything?"

"No, but Beetle will be here also. You must have read about his mother."

"Yes," Maryann said. "How awful."

Susan knew she could count on Maryann to be sympathetic and compassionate. She'd always been. Susan decided to make Maryann's favorite dessert, peanut butter pie.

Monday, Jeff was as businesslike as possible when interacting with his secretary. She returned the behavior. It was as if there had been nothing between them. While he was pleased, he wasn't sure how to take it.

And he was so conflicted inside about what they'd done; he left the office, pretending to have a meeting. Back at his room, he knelt on the floor, sobbing his heart out. "Oh Lord forgive me for I have sinned. I've committed adultery!"

After moments had passed, he was able to get up and splash water on his face and look in the mirror. The shame was almost unbearable. He flashed on thoughts of taking off, leaving everything behind.

At once a peace washed over his anxiousness and he felt forgiven, but had the overwhelming urge to tell Susan and ask her for forgiveness, too. At the same time he felt the urge, he also knew he wasn't ready yet. He was too afraid she'd want nothing to do with him after hearing what he'd done.

I'll find the right moment after she's moved here and some time has passed, he decided.

Natalie caught up to Johnny in the hall at school. "I've been looking all over for you," she said.

He showed no reaction or even that he was paying any attention to her at all.

"Did you hear me?" she spoke louder. "I said…"

"I heard you," he said. "Now if you don't mind, I want to be by myself." He shrugged off the grip she had on his sleeve.

"What's wrong with you?" she asked. "I thought we were back together?"

Johnny breathed in hard, blowing out with a disgusted sound. He stared at her but didn't speak. Then she understood.

"This is about Beetle's mother, isn't it?"

"Uh," he paused. "Yeah, you wouldn't understand."

"The heck I don't!" Natalie's anger and feelings of rejection surfaced. "I understand perfectly! I was a major jerk for taking you back. I don't ever want to see you again." She stormed off down the hall. Johnny didn't follow.

Gordon fumed. He did not want Beetle away from him. How dare that woman think that she can take him away from me, he thought.

His home phone rang. It was Mr. Z. "Can I come by for those children's movies?"

"Children's movies?" he said. "Oh yeah, How about seven?" The thought of a buyer coming over for some of his videos distracted him from feeling so angry.

The table was set with Susan's favorite table settings, milk white dinnerware with tiny pale blue flowers. The sight made her feel like springtime, new beginnings, and peace. She hoped those who would be dining with her would feel good as well.

Natalie is in a strange mood, Susan thought after observing her daughter for a few moments after she came home from school.

"Could you help me, please?" Susan asked her.

"Um huh." Natalie's face was tensed up.

"What's up, Natalie?"

"Nothing," she said, but her face continued to give away that that wasn't true.

"Come on, Nat. I'm a good listener."

"Mom, I don't want to talk about it."

"Okay," Susan backed off.

"What do you want me to help you with?"

Together they brought everything to the table, the stuffed shells, green beans with Parmesan cheese, homemade applesauce, carrot sticks and black olives. Beetle peeked around the corner just as Maryann rang the front door bell.

"Have you ever met Beetle?" Susan asked Maryann.

"I saw you at Mr. Swanson's."

"Oh, yeah," Beetle responded. He turned morbidly blah looking.

"Well, okay," Susan quickly changed the subject. "Let's eat."

Susan sat at one end of the table. Maryann sat at the other, and Beetle and Natalie sat across from one another. Susan smiled at everyone. The fuller table reminded her of when Jeff and Max were home.

"How's school, Natalie?" Maryann displayed her usual interest.

"Boring." Natalie displayed her usual teenage grumpiness.

"How's that boyfriend of yours?" "I don't want to talk about him," Natalie answered, "ever!"

"Did you guys break up?" Beetle got into it.

"I don't want to talk about it!" Natalie took a mouthful of stuffed shells.

"Erowwwwww!" Susan mimicked a catlike sound. "Put away the claws, Natalie. Our guests are simply asking questions. How can we know what is going on with your social life, if we don't ask?"

"Why does everyone want to know?" She rolled her eyes.

"Okay, everyone," Susan stood as if preparing to make a major announcement, "Natalie's social life is off limits tonight," Susan teased. "It is going to be very dull, though, without it."

All but Natalie laughed, even Beetle. Hearing Maryann's sweet laugh made Susan realize how much she was going to miss her. She decided right then that she didn't care if Maryann liked women more than men or apples more than oranges. She's my friend, she thought, and I shall miss her.

The rest of the dinner went smoothly. When Susan served Maryann's favorite dessert, Maryann got teary eyed. "You always remember," she said.

Beetle and Natalie excused themselves from the table and headed for the family room. Beetle said, "Thanks," with a full stomach and hungry eyes. The hungry eyes of a person emotionally starved.

"You are entirely welcome," Susan said. "It was my pleasure." Maryann and Susan cleared the table, and Susan put the teakettle on. After everything was cleared and the tea was poured, they remained in the kitchen, their usual haunt.

"Lots of changes," Maryann began.

"Yup."

"I should feel bad about being pregnant," she said. "But I don't. I've wanted a child for so long."

"Well, now you are going to have one." Susan would love to be honest with her and talk about Gordon, the baby, and her lesbian friend Jill, but she couldn't. Sipping tea and chatting casually was all she could handle that evening. Maybe the words would come another time, she thought.

"How do you really feel about this move?" Maryann asked.

Susan contemplated her answer for a moment, holding her teacup between her two hands. "I feel good about it. It was my idea, after all."

"Oh?"

"Yeah, I'm tired of being apart from Jeff."

"You are the lucky one. You have a great marriage, kids."

"Yes," Susan agreed, "I am lucky, but now you'll have one, too. A kid, that is."

"Yeah." Maryann touched her stomach, and smiled.

They finished their tea, and the phone rang.

"Is Beetle there?"

"Who is this?" Susan asked.

"Mr. Swanson."

"Oh, he's spending the night. Didn't you get the message?"

"Can I speak to him?"

"I'm sorry, he's busy." She lied, sort of. But she didn't want the man near Beetle, anymore.

"Tell him I called." His tone was arrogant and cold.

"Good bye."

Susan shivered.

"Was it him?" Maryann asked.

"Yeah, I hate the son of a…"

Maryann looked down, as if ashamed. "Like I said, I should hate the guy, but I can't because of the baby."

Chapter 17

"We've got enough now to arrest him," Detective Wallace said to the other detectives in the room.

"So why don't we?" one asked.

He shook his head. "I want Swanson sent away for a long time and you all know these guys get off easy. It makes me sick."

"What are we waiting for?" another asked.

"It would be good if we could get one of his victims to testify, but so far they don't want to get involved. They are either in denial or embarrassed."

"What about this Beetle kid?"

"I don't know if he's been involved in porno activities yet. I have a feeling Swanson is getting him ready, but nothing has happened."

"I'll call that woman whose daughter is friends with the kid, and see what anyone knows."

Susan wasn't thrilled about going to the station again.

"What do you want?" she asked Detective Wallace.

"What can you tell me about Beetle's activities?"

"Not much." She told about Beetle spending the night and Swanson's unhappiness with it.

"Let him go back there," said Detective Wallace. "We need his help."

Susan was shocked. "I'm doing everything I can to keep him away!"

"Please?"

"I don't want that boy involved."

"He's already involved."

"No!"

"Then you won't help us?"

"I guess not."

"You are interfering with police work, you realize." The detective had a stern look on his face.

"I'm thinking of the boy, that's all."

"But there are many boys who have already been involved."

Susan looked him dead in the eyes, and said, "Well, maybe this one can be saved."

"You must continue to keep quiet about this," ordered Wallace. "You'll do that much, won't you?"

"Of course, Detective."

"Well, I guess you are free to leave."

"Okay."

Feeling powerful, having just stood up to the police, something she would never have imagined she'd do, she drove back home to watch her afternoon soaps. "Nothing like watching 'soaps' to get away from it all."

Jeff wondered what his secretary was up to. He knew why he was acting so businesslike around her. He wanted to pretend nothing had ever happened between them. But what was going on with her, he wondered.

"Your wife called," she said.

"My wife?"

"Yes, she told me they are moving here."

"Yes, they are. I'm so pleased."

"I told her maybe I could take your daughter under my wing and show her around, you know, the mall…"

"No," he interrupted.

"No?"

"I mean, um, you needn't worry about them."

"I'm just trying to be friendly."

"I know, but that's okay."

"About that day," she started.

"Let's never mention that, ever," he gave a serious look. She giggled. Then she went right back to what she was working on at the computer.

Jeff had to leave the office again. He was about to be ill. Guilt was doing a number on his body.

"Mom, you'll never guess what happened!" Natalie was bubbly upon arriving home, for a change.

"What? What happened?"

"Beetle is going out with one of the twins. He's going there for dinner tonight."

"You're kidding."

"No, isn't that awesome? I didn't think those girls were into guys, but I guess so. She asked him out. Can you believe it?"

"That's nice."

"He's never had a girlfriend," Natalie continued. "He's like, so goofy, it's adorable. He's asking me all these questions about stuff."

"How sweet."

"Oh, and he said that Mr. Swanson is working on taking him in legally as a foster child or something. Isn't that neat?"

Susan could fake it no longer. "No it isn't! I'll never let that happen!"

Natalie looked stunned. "Why, Mom?"

"I...I...I just think he'd be better off with someone else. Don't ask me why."

"I've never seen you like this. What is it, Mom? After

all, we're moving, remember?"

"I know. Just never mind."

"I can't wait to move," said Natalie.

"What?" Susan couldn't believe what she was hearing.

"No, I'm not sick. I want to move. I hate it here," Natalie said.

"Because of Johnny?"

"It's a lot of stuff. Hey, could we find that house again?"

"What house?"

"The one we got stuck in the mud near."

"Oh, I get it. That cute guy, right?" Susan smiled.

"You got it." Natalie playfully pointed a finger at her mother.

And Susan was beginning to get it. Life goes on. It doesn't matter about a lot of things. Things can get better even mother and daughter things.

"I love you, Nat."

"I love you, too, Mom."

Jeff had difficulty getting to sleep. He was ashamed of having had sex with his secretary and scared that Susan would find out. He couldn't fire the woman, because she'd talk. He stared at the ceiling. He didn't know what to do.

He was so ashamed, "Lord, what is wrong with me?"

Jeff decided he would have to tell Susan before they moved. He figured he owed her that much. That way if she couldn't forgive him and live with it, she'd at least have an out. I hate myself, he thought.

Susan rushed over to Maryann's. She had sounded terrible on the phone. Fluffy yipped at her, which was nothing new.

"Maryann, I'm here," she greeted once inside the door.

"I'm in bed," Maryann's voice sounded awful.

She looked pale.

"What's the matter?"

Her lips trembled as she cried. "I lost it."

Susan knew at once that she must have miscarried the baby. She hurried to the side of the bed, and sat down. Holding Maryann's head in her arms, she hugged her tightly. Instinctively, she rocked slowly. She petted her hair, and then she wept.

"It's okay," Susan whispered. Maryann tried to talk, but Susan shushed her. "We'll talk later." Maryann eventually fell to sleep in Susan's arms.

The service was brief. Beetle had a handful of relatives, who couldn't have been more distant. It was awkward. When Susan observed Swanson assuming the role of guardian, she wanted to throw up.

Susan daydreamed about Maryann taking Beetle into her home. He wasn't a baby, but he was a kid in need of a home. Hmm, she wondered.

Seeing Detective Wallace show up at the service confused Susan. What was going on? He smiled a don't-act-like-you-know-me smile, to which Susan looked the other way.

When the service was over, and people were leaving the funeral parlor, a group of men descended upon Mr. Swanson. He struggled, but ended up in handcuffs and an embarrassed looking face. Beetle shouted at the group as they hauled Swanson away.

Susan rushed to Beetle's side. "It's okay, Beetle," she said. "Come with me."

"What is going on? Why are they taking him away?"

"I can't say right now, but soon you'll find out that he wasn't who he appeared to be."

Beetle shook his head and remained silent. He followed

Susan to her car.

"Why don't you stay with us until we move, then we'll make another arrangement?" Susan attempted a conversation.

"Don't take this wrong," said Beetle, "but I'm about to take off right now. I'm really pissed off!"

"Take it easy, Beetle."

His hands were nervously rubbing his pant leg and he really did look like he was ready to bolt.

"Why not come to the house and try to relax," Susan offered. "I'll tell you what I know about Swanson. Is that a deal?"

Beetle said nothing. He stared out the side window of the car as they drove to the house.

Susan suggested he watch TV in the family room, thought that maybe he'd need some time alone.

Later, when Natalie arrived home from school, Susan told her to visit with Beetle.

"He's gone!" Natalie yelled from the family room.

A blanket of fear mixed with sadness shrouded mother and daughter.

"I'm worried, Mom," said Natalie.

"Me, too," said Susan. "Me, too." Life isn't always fair, she thought.

The police were alerted to Beetle's unknown whereabouts after twenty-four hours had passed. Susan hated to do it, knowing that Social Services would more than likely have to get involved and then who knows where he'd end up.

Natalie was depressed. She was consumed with worry over Beetle. "Let's pray, Natalie," Susan suggested.

"Dear Lord, we need special prayers for Beetle. He's been through so many difficult times lately, and has never had it very easy." Susan paused, collecting her thoughts. "Please watch over him, and help him find a good home and happiness. Amen."

"Amen," echoed Natalie. "Thanks, Mom." The pair hugged.

Chapter 18

Jeff pulled his car into the driveway. He was gathering the courage to confess his infidelity to his wife and use the weekend to do whatever it took to beg her forgiveness and convince her that he was worth staying with. He was more nervous than he'd ever been in his life.

The news was on, and the ladies were glued to the TV set.

"Hello," Jeff called out.

Susan ran to her husband and buried her face into his shoulder, crying from the strain of the week's events.

"My goodness," he pulled away for a moment. "What is it?"

Susan recapped about Swanson's arrest, her knowledge about the case, and Beetle's disappearance.

"Wow! A guy can miss a lot in a week."

"Yeah, but hopefully you missed me the most." Susan was eager to be alone with Jeff.

"You bet I did." Jeff surrounded her with his arms and snuggled in close. He wasn't sure if he could dump his ugly confession on her this weekend, now that he'd heard all that she had on her mind. Better wait, he thought. Cowardly, yes, he knew, but he also wanted the time to be right for telling her.

Maryann sat in a chair, feeling as depressed as she ever had. Her legs wouldn't work. She felt as if she couldn't walk, didn't want to. The loss of the baby cinched it for her. She really wasn't worthy. She really wasn't capable of being truly happy, she thought.

The knock at the door surprised her. She tried to get up off the chair, but her legs went dead and she fell down. "Just a minute," she yelled. Fluffy was leaping and yipping at her, nervous and excited. She gathered up her strength and got to her feet. Upon opening the door, she gasped. Beetle was standing there.

"May I come in?"

"Well, of course," she widened the door opening.

"I saw you come here," he said, "so I knew where you lived."

"Oh," Maryann was more curious than she'd ever been in her life.

"I was thinking," he said. "Well, since you live alone, maybe I could stay here."

Maryann stiffened. Her strength was regained immediately. Her heart raced. "Stay here?"

"Well, if it's okay."

"Okay?" Maryann began to laugh. She could not believe it. It was a miracle, she thought. "I would be honored."

Beetle walked into her home and into her heart forever.

Susan was thrilled with the news that Beetle had showed up at Maryann's. She helped them work on setting up guardianship. Helping them kept her occupied when she wasn't packing to move.

They'd found a buyer for their house and moving day was fast approaching. One evening Susan slipped over to Maryann's for a visit, knowing it would be one of their last visits before the move.

"How does Fluffy like having Beetle here?" Susan asked.

"She took to him right away," Maryann answered.

"That dirty dog, she likes everyone but me."

"Well, I like ya," Maryann laughed Susan's favorite laugh, then she wiped a tear from rolling down her cheek, also realizing it was one of their last times to be together. "Whom will you gripe to about Natalie?" she asked.

"I don't know," Susan returned. "Maybe we'll finally get along better. Then she laughed. "You'll probably be the one who'll call me up all the time asking parenting questions about Beetle."

Maryann smiled. "You've got a point there. But I suspect that little girlfriend of his is planning to keep him pretty busy. He's already talking about activities at church and going to church camp this summer."

"That's wonderful."

Then Maryann turned serious. "Susan, I feel like I should tell you something," she said. "Something I've wanted to tell you for years."

"It doesn't matter," Susan interjected. Maryann looked into Susan's eyes and then Maryann realized that Susan already knew. She must have been the one who'd contacted Jill, Maryann thought.

"I…" Maryann began.

"Like I said," Susan cut in. "It doesn't matter."

They stood up and hugged long and meaningfully.

"I'll miss you my friend." Maryann said.

"I'll miss you, too."

"Don't jump in any puddles," Maryann said as they finished their hug.

"Oh, you'd be surprised about me," Susan smiled. "I'm into that sort of thing, now." Maryann's laugh followed Susan out the door and all the way home.

Jeff nervously adjusted his tie. The Board Meeting he'd

been to had been a tough one, lots of issues. His uneasiness with not telling Susan yet hadn't helped, so he made yet another new decision to take the ugly secret to his grave.

"This will have to be my cross to bear," he spoke out loud. He was too afraid of the possible negative consequences that may occur after telling. Things were too good. The family was moving soon, the job was going okay, and he expected it to go even better after Susan lived there.

His secretary hadn't been coming on to him lately, so he figured it was over. She must have gotten the hint.

Chapter 19

It was not easy hauling out twenty years of accumulation. Susan went through the boxes in the attic, trying to weed out some of the stuff.

A doll that Natalie had never played with. "Maybe I'll have a granddaughter someday who will love dolls." So it stayed.

A box of curtains she hadn't used in at least fifteen years. "Good Will donation."

The job took all day, and very little was weeded out. "Oh, well," Susan sighed. "We'll just drag it all to the next place, what's the difference?"

Natalie was into the move like she was into life. It'll happen, and she'll go along, but she wasn't miserable or enthusiastic about it, either. At least we aren't fighting every minute, Susan thought.

Max hadn't been thrilled about the move. He wasn't home very often, but home was still "home." And unlike Natalie, who could make new friends, he felt he wouldn't have time to and wasn't interested, anyway.

"I think I'll live at college this summer," he told his parents. "I'll get a job and just stay."

The news hurt Susan's feelings, but she tried to understand. She was noticing that once they've been on their own, they are different. It is hard to "go home" after being "on your own."

"So many changes," Susan sighed as she packed up the

last box. The movers would be moving them the next day.

"Good bye old house," she said. No emotion overcame her. She just wanted to get on with it.

Setting up the new house was exciting and fun for Susan. Moving the furniture around to find a good place for it all was challenging. The wallpaper and painted walls were complimentary to what they had. And Susan was never fussy about that sort of thing, so it really didn't matter, anyway.

Once the place was looking like "home" she settled into her usual routine. Longing for normalcy, she looked in the phone book for doctors, dentists, and churches. She wanted to plunge right into the business of 'living.'

Then the hole developed; the hole in her stomach. It felt like a rat had gnawed on her insides. 'Home' didn't come as easily as she'd figured it would. Trying to find new doctors, dentists, and a possible church made the hole even bigger. The only thing that helped was watching the soaps in the afternoon. Susan looked forward to the afternoon.

Natalie loved the new school. She had a smile on her face every morning, and upon returning home afterward. Susan was delighted for her.

Jeff bounced around like a boy with a new bike for Christmas. He grinned all the time. And yet even so, the hole kept getting deeper inside Susan.

She decided to pop in to Jeff's office unannounced one day, feeling depressed over the hole.

"I don't know what is wrong with me," she said.

"Honey, it's okay," Jeff assured her. "You lived in one place for twenty years. You're probably going through separation or grief or something. It's normal."

Susan noticed her period was late. It had never been late, except for twice, when she was pregnant. "Oh my God!"

She found a gynecologist and made an appointment.

"You aren't pregnant," the woman gynecologist told her, after the exam was complete. "It could be the move, or premenopause."

"Menopause?" Susan hadn't given that a thought.

The hole widened more. She had to start filling it, or fear that it would eventually make her disappear.

Jeff was more and more uncomfortable about his cheating. His secretary seemed to not be interested, and onto other males in the building. She was flirty and self confident. Jeff was glad she wasn't tempting him anymore. That made it a little better, but there was still the guilt.

Every time he was close to Susan he felt guilty. He almost couldn't look her in the eyes. He hated himself for what he'd done. "How could I?" he asked himself that question several times each day. And now that Susan seemed to be depressed, he hated himself more. "How can I tell her, now?" He again decided to not tell.

Jeff's secretary got a kick out of Jeff acting nervous around her, now that they'd had sex. "It's so cute," she thought. She didn't care if they "did it" again or not. She had so many guys in mind to "do it" with. There was that "hunk" of a custodian, she'd noticed pushing a sweeper, and one of the Math teachers and, so many.

"I think I'll get to know Jeff's family, though," she thought. She really hoped to see him squirm a little. "What a kick," she giggled to herself.

Natalie spotted the young man who had pulled their car out of the mud, the first day she attended the new school. And he had spotted her. Daniel was polite and attentive, the complete personality opposite of Johnny. And she liked his looks, too. He was more the sunny, handsome type then the dark brooding hunk type that had attracted her to Johnny.

Daniel began inviting Natalie over to the farm on a frequent basis. His mother, Rachel, called Susan to welcome her to the community.

"Would you like to come out to visit?" she asked.

"I'd love to," said Susan.

Susan hoped that the new friend would help to fill the hole. She missed Maryann. She stopped by the school to tell Jeff about her plans.

"Hello Susan," Jeff's secretary greeted. "Welcome to town."

"Well, thank you."

"I'd like to have you all over for dinner to my apartment soon."

"That would be lovely."

Jeff breezed into the office from the hallway. "What are you doing, Susan?"

"I stopped by to tell you I'm going to Daniel's to visit his mother."

"Oh, that'll be fun for you." He glanced nervously around.

"I told Susan I'd like to have your family over for dinner," his secretary said. "To my apartment."

Jeff furrowed his forehead and didn't comment.

"Dear," he said. "Come into my office for a minute." Susan followed him into his office.

Jeff cleared his throat several times, and spoke just above a whisper, "Don't accept," he said.

"What?"

"Don't accept an invitation, I don't want to mix business with personal stuff."

"Well, okay," Susan agreed. "If that's what you want."

She was puzzled though, by his reaction to a possible dinner invitation from his secretary.

"I don't want her to get the wrong idea."

Then Susan got it. She had observed women noticing her husband all through the years. It made her feel good; knowing that he was hers.

"Hey, good looking," she teased. "I'm the only one who's going to feed you." They smiled, and Susan made the move to leave, not wanting to take up too much of his time. She'd always respected that he was working and she wasn't going to be one of those wives who hung around their husband's work site.

Jeff felt ill again after she kissed him good bye and left. He felt guilty as hell.

Susan suspected that Rachel had not only been thoughtful about inviting her over because she was new to the area, but because she somehow knew that Susan needed a friend.

"It's not easy moving," Rachel began, after seating Susan in her large eat-in kitchen.

"No," Susan agreed, "It sure isn't. Especially after living in the same place for twenty years."

"Well, everyone is very pleased with your husband here, so maybe you'll be here for the next twenty years."

"How long have you lived here?"

Rachel looked about the room, decorated so plainly, yet it was pleasant to be in, and said, "I grew up on this farm."

"Oh my," said Susan.

"My husband and I bought it from my parents after they'd had enough of farming."

"That's so wonderful."

"Is it?" Rachel said.

"Well, yes."

Rachel again looked around the room, and said, "Sometimes I wish I'd been an Army brat and moved around all my life." She laughed.

Susan laughed, too. She already liked this down to earth farm friend, and was looking forward to future get togethers with her.

Natalie and Daniel walked down the hallway arm in arm. Their mutual admiration was obvious.

"Want to come over after school?" he said.

"Why not come to my house this time?" Natalie asked.

"I'd love to."

Natalie was enjoying this new, peacefully happy relationship. She loved Daniel's playful, yet gentlemanly attitude towards her.

"I think you should get to know some of the girls at school, too," Daniel said.

"Why?" Natalie never cared much for hanging around girls, always preferred the guys.

"I just think it would be good for you."

"Okay."

"I'll bring Jen and Shana, too. We've grown up together and they've been wanting to get to know you."

"Whatever you want." Natalie didn't care what he did, as long as he kept coming around. She adored him.

Jeff noticed his secretary bending over her desk again, as if she'd lost yet another contact. "I've got to get her out of here," he mumbled soft enough so she could not hear.

The ugly snake of temptation reared its head again, seeing her sprawled out and he mumbled, "Lead me not into temptation, but deliver me from evil." The Lord's Prayer had always been his source of comfort during needy times. He'd been praying it daily since his "mistake."

Jeff quickly left the office and continued down the hall, feeling frustrated with his situation and distraught over what to do.

Susan and Rachel walked out to Susan's car, with a plan to get together at Susan's next.

"See you Friday," Susan called out as she left the driveway to travel home. The hole seemed smaller, but not filled in yet.

"Thank you, Lord," Susan said. "You knew I needed a friend."

The ride was sweet and comforting. Moving had been harder than she'd anticipated. Being with Jeff was worth it, though, she thought.

Chapter 20

"I had sex with another person," Jeff announced over morning coffee to his wife.

Susan sat perfectly still and stared. He could have been speaking a foreign language for all she knew. In her experience the words he spoke were out of the realm of possible word combinations he could have ever put together to say to her.

Natalie was spending the weekend with Jen at Shana's house. They'd met and hit it off right away. Jeff and Susan were delighted that she'd finally clicked with some girlfriends. Of course, Daniel and some other guys were going to be around that weekend, too.

Jeff had decided five seconds before he spoke those words, to make his confession. He couldn't live with the lie any longer. He wanted to have the weekend to beg her forgiveness.

"If this is your idea of a joke," Susan said. "I don't find anything funny about it."

"It's not a joke." Jeff looked at his wife with pathetic eyes, eyes tearing up with sadness.

"Oh my God." Susan wept. Jeff wept, too.

After they calmed down, Susan wanted some answers. "Who did you have sex with?"

"I don't want to say." Jeff hung his head. "I just hope someday you can forgive me. I'm so sorry and so ashamed of myself."

"What do you mean, you don't want to say?" Susan yelled.

"I'm so disgusted, I don't want to talk about it."

"Well, too bad. You lost certain rights when you decided to be unfaithful to me."

Jeff wanted to take off; he was more uncomfortable than he'd imagined he'd be. He could tell by Susan's tone that this was not going to be easy, and he doubted at that moment that she would ever be able to forgive him.

"To be honest, I'm embarrassed and just don't want to give details. It's bad enough that I strayed."

Susan began hitting him on the shoulder. "How could you do this?" She kept hitting him. "How could you do this to me?"

"I'm so sorry. I hate myself."

Susan stormed out of the room to the bathroom, where she shut the door and bawled for a long time.

Jeff left the house. He contemplated taking off. He was so upset with himself. He couldn't live with what he'd done to Susan. "I am scum," he said. He drove for hours all around, trying to figure out what he'd do. He wanted to drive off the road, but didn't have the guts. "I'm a coward," he said aloud.

He drove back to the house, planning to beg Susan to forgive him. And if she wouldn't, he'd offer to move out. He'd go back to the boarding house or something.

Susan rushed to the door, when he arrived. She was crying, had been for hours. "How could you?" she greeted him. Jeff wanted to hold her, but didn't; he didn't want to offend her.

"Why won't you tell me who?"

"I am too ashamed."

"Why did you do it?"

"All I can say is that I was flattered that she wanted me, and I did a stupid thing."

"Flattered?"

"I don't know why, Susan."

"I just can't believe this," she screamed. "I never imagined this would happen to us." She shook her head back and forth.

"You probably won't believe me," said Jeff, "but I never did either."

"Well then why did it?"

Jeff couldn't say, because he didn't know, either.

The rest of the evening they were silent.

At bedtime, Jeff offered to sleep on the couch. Susan burst into tears. "Is that what you think I want?"

"I just don't want to hurt you more."

Susan threw herself at him. "I want to be held, I'm falling apart."

Jeff held her tightly, relieved to be asked to. He felt hopeful. Just maybe, he thought. Maybe she can forgive me.

They ended up lying down. Susan almost desperately wanted Jeff to make love to her. She had to feel needed and wanted. She was hurt, wounded. She ached to have him love her.

She kissed his mouth hard, forced her body against his, pushing and pushing. He felt so sorry for her, he knew she was so angry with him. He could tell by her actions. She was always so gentle and sweet in bed. But he went along. He'd done enough damage. He would let her lead from now on.

After making love, they fell asleep.

First thing the next morning, Susan started in again.

"You have to tell me about it. I have a right to know."

"I'm so ashamed." Jeff looked away from his wife of twenty-five years and then slowly began the ugly story telling. He left nothing out.

Susan looked as if she was about to vomit.

"I don't know what to say or do," she said. "I don't know anything about this stuff." Tears came again.

"Susan, I love you. I'm sorry. All I ask is that maybe, just maybe you can forgive me someday."

"That little bitch!"

"I know," Jeff consoled. "I'm so sorry."

"I can't do this!" she screamed. "I'm never going to be okay!"

Susan ran to the bathroom for another session of bawling.

Jeff sat on the couch and stared.

Chapter 21

Natalie and friends spent the evening playing board games, laughing and joking. It was good for Natalie, who'd forgotten how special girlfriends can be. It had been a few years since she'd had any.

"So, what was that Johnny like?" asked Shana.

"At first it was like I couldn't imagine ever being with anyone else," Natalie explained, "but then it became creepier and creepier as I got to really know him."

"Ooh," said Jen. "What do you mean, was he like a stalker or a vampire?" After which she giggled, "Come on tell us."

Natalie giggled, too. She almost wished he'd been a vampire. At least it would be more exciting to talk about then his being a cheating, inconsiderate jerk.

"No," said Natalie. "I don't want to even think about that jerk ever again. So tell me about Daniel. Has he had a lot of girlfriends?"

Jen and Shana smiled at each other. "Well if you aren't going to give us any juicy details about this Johnny, we might as well tell you that Mr. Daniel is a perfect gentleman, a 'saint' really," said Jen.

"He's never had a girlfriend, just really good friends," said Shana, "like us, and we think it is adorable that he is so ga ga over you."

They all giggled then, and Natalie felt as if her insides had flipped over. She was overjoyed that Daniel was the way he was. She felt honored, happy, and just plain lucky.

Her smile remained for the rest of the evening, a permanent fixture for all to see. She was a picture of contentment.

Susan wanted to leave, but couldn't. She couldn't let on to Natalie that anything was wrong. She just wanted the whole thing to be not true. But it was.

When Natalie arrived home from her sleep over weekend, she only saw two parents who'd always seemed crazy about each other. Her "rocks" were in place. Her "perfect" family was intact. Susan and Jeff were performing the acting jobs of their lives.

"Did you have a good time, dear?" Susan asked her daughter.

"I had a blast!" Natalie raised up, as if she was about to do a cheerleading number.

Susan felt good inside for her daughter. At least Natalie is finally happy, she thought. The fake outside smile was painful, but necessary to maintain. Susan always did the "right" thing. She wasn't about to "go off" now. Even if she did feel distraught, miserable, and angrier than she'd ever felt she was capable of feeling.

She wanted to take a baseball bat and shove it up Jeff's secretary's private parts. She had no idea she could feel that violent, that enraged, but she did.

When she watched shows on TV and saw women getting so angry with their partner's mistresses, she'd always been amused at how they could get so angry with them. Now I know, she thought. Now I know.

Monday morning was awkward. Jeff was going to tell his secretary that Susan knew about what they'd done. He was so guilty and ashamed that he didn't want to go to work.

"Susan knows," was all he said to her. His secretary looked like she was going to pass out.

"I can't believe you told her," she said. "Why?"

"I love my wife. I couldn't live a lie."

"I need the day off," she said.

"Fine."

Susan set about the task of getting through the day. It was all different, now. Before the confession, she had bad days, occasionally, but now she had dreadful days. Days of darkness, and dark thoughts.

That hole that seemed to want to fill up was larger than ever. It was a deep pit, consuming her every thought and idea.

The phone rang and it was Rachel asking her to come over for a visit. Susan wanted to say "no" but she knew it would be good for her. She had to carry on. She had to do the "right thing," as always.

She decided to stop by to tell Jeff, and face his secretary. She figured she'd get that over with as soon as possible. When she entered the parking lot, his secretary was headed for her car. She saw Susan, and appeared visibly uncomfortable, directed her glances downward and quickly ducked into her car and sped off.

Susan wanted to feel like running her over, but instead she felt a flood of pity. The woman appeared remorseful, or at least guilty. She looked like a mess. Susan decided to send her a note expressing her feelings of forgiveness.

After all, she thought, I've been trained all my life at church to forgive. I guess now I'm being put to the test.

When Jeff saw Susan, he was terrified. He had no idea if they would be able to get through this or not.

"Good morning," Susan greeted.

"Good morning," Jeff returned.

"I saw her."

"You…"

"I'm going to send her a note that says I forgive you," Susan told him.

Jeff stared. He could hardly believe what he'd heard. A smile overcame his face. "You are amazing." He continued to stare at this woman he'd spent twenty-five years with. He thought he knew her, but discovered right then that she could still surprise him. "I don't know what to say. I'm completely blown away. You are unbelievable. Hmm hmm."

"She looked so uncomfortable, I felt sorry for her."

That did it! Jeff felt even worse. How could I have betrayed this remarkable woman? he thought. I really am scum. He kept his thoughts to himself and just thanked God he was blessed with such a beautiful wonderful wife. Tears filled his eyes. He reached out his arms, hoping to get a hug, but still insecure about offending her with any physical advances. Susan walked slowly, until she was close enough to fall into his waiting arms. "I love you so much," he whispered.

"I love you, too," she whispered back.

The next few weeks were like a honeymoon for Jeff and Susan. They dripped affection, were even more attentive than ever to each other, and worked at pretending "it" had never happened.

Chapter 22

Max had definitely decided to stay at college when the semester was over. Susan understood, but it saddened her. It was just one more thing for her to deal with. And yet she was relieved because she realized that she wouldn't have to "pretend" around him if he did come home.

"I'm fine until I picture them together," she said aloud. The images of Jeff and his secretary having sex put her into a deep depression. She was okay until the images appeared in her head.

Jeff felt like a new man. He was disgusted by what he'd done, but the guilt had been lessened considerably after confessing to Susan, and seeing how unbelievably forgiving she'd been about it. He conducted himself in a professional manner, as did his secretary. It was almost as if "it" had never happened.

Rachel barely knew Susan, but sensed sadness about her and one day when they were visiting; she invited her minister over to join them.

"I'd like you to meet Pastor Bob," she introduced him to Susan.

"Pastor, this is our principal's wife, Susan. She just moved to the district."

Pastor Bob had been at the church for several years and was well liked. His wife had passed away two years before after suffering for years with cancer.

"Nice to meet you," Susan said.

"Nice to meet you, too."

They all enjoyed brownies and instant cappuccinos around the kitchen table. Rachel and Pastor Bob invited Susan and family to attend church the next Sunday. She agreed, wondering if she really would, though. She felt so down lately, she didn't know if she had the interest or energy to commit to church participation.

Pastor Bob asked for her address so that he might stop by to meet Jeff and Natalie. Susan didn't see any reason to say, "no," other than her blase attitude.

Before leaving Rachel's, Susan extended her hand to shake the minister's. He looked at her and said, "I'm really delighted to know you." His free hand covered her extended one, sandwiching hers between both of his, making it a warmer shake. She desperately appreciated the attention.

The knock on the door in the middle of her soaps the next day, surprised her. No one had come to the door unexpectedly during the day since they'd moved in. Pastor Bob extended his right arm with a handful of fresh-cut flowers in it. "Housewarming gesture," he explained.

"Oh!" Susan felt awkward. "But Jeff and Natalie aren't here."

"I figured," the pastor stepped inside the opened door. "I just wanted to be nice. Flowers are a nice touch, don't you think?"

Susan figured he wanted to visit, so she said the appropriate thing, "Would you like to sit down?"

"Well," he hesitated. "If you aren't busy."

Susan took the flowers from him and headed for the kitchen to find a vase. "Thanks for the flowers," she said as she trailed off.

Pastor Bob followed her to the kitchen, instead of

taking a seat. He startled her.

"Oh, um," Susan stammered.

"This is a nice home," he said.

"Yes it is."

"Have you lived in a lot of places?"

"Actually, no. We just moved from a home we'd lived in for twenty years."

"Wow! I've moved around most of my adult life. In the ministry there is a lot of movement."

"I imagine there probably is," Susan wasn't used to having a man visit. She wondered what to do. Should I offer tea, say I have to go out to do errands? She felt uneasy. She also noticed herself noticing the way his smile ended in dimples and his eyes lit up when he spoke.

"Are you a homemaker?" he asked.

"Yes."

"That is remarkable."

"What do you mean?"

"There are so few women anymore who seem content or willing to choose the home as a career." He did the dimples and eye thing again.

Susan felt warm, appreciated, and a little too needy of his attention, but it felt wonderful.

"Thank you." She moved towards the refrigerator, stumbling a little over a sticky patch in the flooring. She chuckled softly. "Hmm, can I get you a cold drink?" She didn't want to take time for a hot beverage. She figured that would take too long and she was way too unnerved by his presence as it was.

"A glass of water would be great."

She ran the faucet while walking to the freezer to get some ice cubes. Pastor Bob met her at the freezer, and leaned over the door as if to take a peek or want to help with the ice cube tray. Susan almost jumped back. She was nervous about his physical closeness.

His laugh brought the dimples and the sparkly eyes. He could sense her nervousness. "Don't have many visitors?" he teased.

"How could you tell?"

"I'm in so many homes, my being a minister," he said.

"It's a thing you can sense."

"No, I don't."

"No, you don't?"

"I don't have many visitors."

"And then there is your husband, who is with people all day, right?"

Susan knew all too well that he was with people all day. Her depression slipped in with the thought of one person in particular he has to be with.

Again, the minister picked up on her uneasiness. "Is there anything I can pray about with you?" he asked.

Susan looked puzzled and even more nervous with his suggestion.

"I mean, after all it is my job."

She again looked puzzled.

"You know," he searched her face to make eye contact, "I'm a minister," he laughed, "that's what I do…pray."

"Oh, thank you, but no, I'm fine, thanks." Susan handed him the water.

"I appreciate it," he said. "If you change your mind let me know."

"Change my mind?"

"You know, about me praying."

"Oh, okay."

He smiled a smile at her that made Susan blush.

That evening Susan told Jeff about the visit from the minister.

"Do you want to try that church?" Jeff asked. He wanted to do anything to make his wife happier and more at peace. "You loved your church involvement before we moved."

Susan nodded her head, but for more than her enjoying church involvement. She already looked forward to more encounters with Pastor Bob.

"So is the guy okay?"

Susan daydreamed a little, "Okay? Yeah, sure. Yeah, he's okay."

"Then that's that, we'll go this Sunday."

Chapter 23

Natalie was thrilled about the idea of going to the church that Daniel and his mother attended. It was just one more opportunity to be with him. Jen and Shana also attended.

"Cool," she said when Susan told her. "Daniel said his minister is awesome."

Susan thought so, too, but didn't think it appropriate to say.

"Well, it looks like we've got a new church," Jeff chimed in.

Susan smiled with the secret thought that she was grateful for more than a place to worship God in. The minister made her feel attractive and wanted.

Max called to let them know he'd be up for the weekend. He didn't want to live there but he did want to see them. Susan was thrilled. She had something else to look forward to along with church.

"You are happy, aren't you?" Jeff asked.

"Yes, I'm having a good week."

"Nothing makes me happier than to see you happy," Jeff touched her shoulders. "You know that, don't you?"

"I do," she answered, "but I still don't understand why you..." she trailed off.

"I don't either," he said. "I'm so sorry."

The tender moment he'd attempted turned gray with the mention of his cheating.

He pulled her to him. "I'm so, so sorry," he whispered

into her hair.

Susan whimpered, tears staining his shirt. He held her for a long time, not wanting to abandon her again in any way. He knew in his heart that it would take time. He knew in his heart he would be there forever for her. He hated himself for hurting her.

Max arrived Friday evening, but not alone. He had a girl with him. Susan felt strange. "Why hadn't he said something?" she asked Jeff.

"They make a handsome couple," Susan said to Jeff as the two walked towards the front of the house.

"You know I've always appreciated mixed couples." Jeff commented on the obvious, that Max and his girl were from different races.

"I just wish he'd said something," Susan said. She was experiencing some awkwardness with Max bringing a girl to the house. She'd always felt that way about her son's love interests even when he was in elementary school. It was a mother-son thing.

They came through the door giggling. "Hi Mom and Dad," Max greeted. "This is Hayley. We go to school together."

Hayley stared, and waited.

"Welcome, Hayley," Jeff was first to speak. He appeared struck by her beauty. She looked about six feet tall and in excellent physical condition.

Susan experienced another twang of uneasiness with Jeff's friendliness towards their son's friend. One of the consequences of cheating is the resulting mistrust and insecurities it produces in the one cheated on.

"Thank you," Hayley returned.

"Nice to meet you," Susan managed to be polite and sociable.

Hayley smiled. Max was smiling, too.

"I should have told you she was coming, but it was all kind of last minute," Max explained. "I hope you don't mind."

Natalie came down the stairs at that point and was all smiles, too.

"Hey big brother!"

"Hey Nat. This is Hayley."

"Hey."

"Hey," called out Hayley. Then they were all smiling.

"Max, you want Hayley to sleep in my room?" Natalie offered.

"Yeah," he answered. "Is that okay with you, Hayley?"

Susan wanted to roll her eyes, but resisted. Is that okay, she mocked her son in her head. Blech! Why couldn't he have stayed a little boy all his life?

"Sure, Max," Hayley reassured her worried beau.

"We can go out with Daniel later."

"Who's Daniel?" Max asked.

"Your sister's special friend," Jeff answered with a teasing tone.

"Ooh!"

"Is anyone hungry?" Susan interrupted the plan making.

All eyes turned to look at her. And all heads nodded "yes."

The group adjourned to the dining room to get to know each other. Susan served submarine sandwiches, chips, a relish tray and homemade chocolate chip cookies.

Later after the kids went out, Susan and Jeff sat in the living room watching TV.

"She seems crazy about our son," said Jeff.

"She sure does," Susan agreed with a sarcastic tone.

"What? Don't you like her?"

"I don't know," Susan answered, then squinted her eyes, "but it's obvious that you do."

"Well," choked Jeff, knowing he had to watch every word he said. He really didn't want to upset her in any way anymore. "She's attractive and seems smart."

"Ummm!" Susan looked like she was going to explode.

"I suppose you want her, too!"

"Susan!" Jeff was shocked. "Come on. What is that about?"

"You know what it's about!" Susan yelled. Then the tears came again. She got up and headed for the bathroom. Jeff felt sick and sad, wondered what to do whether to follow her in there or give her her space. He gave her her space.

Chapter 24

Getting everyone ready to leave for church was more difficult. Two more in the bathroom, etc. When they were ready, they piled into the family car.

"I'll be getting my permit to drive soon," said Natalie.

"Don't remind us," teased Jeff. Her sixteenth birthday was approaching, and she'd already been nagging about getting her permit to learn to drive as soon as she blew out the sixteen candles she'd have on her cake.

"I'm not taking her driving," said Max. Hayley snuggled into his arm and laughed.

"I'm not," added Susan.

Natalie pouted and said, "Thanks a lot guys!"

"Oh princess, you know I will," Jeff reassured her.

"My little princess," mocked Max. Hayley laughed again.

Susan thought it was sweet that Hayley was in tune with Max. She figured if he had to have a girlfriend, he'd better have one who was crazy about him. She turned to look at the three of them in the back seat and smiled their way.

"What? Mom," Max asked.

"Nothin' Just glad to have you around." She turned back to face front. Jeff glanced her way. Susan smiled at him and slipped her hand in his across the front seat. Jeff breathed an obvious sigh of relief. He knew he'd have to be patient. Her healing would take time. And he'd give her all the time she needed.

Pastor Bob noticed Susan and family glided into the church pew. He was thrilled to see her again. Since his wife had died he'd had his lonely spells. A visit with a nice woman was appreciated.

"I was watching a TV show the other day and they said that 50% of men and women cheat on their spouses!" Pastor Bob opened his sermon.

"They say that it used to be 50% for men and only about 10% for women, but now it is even. Can you believe it?"

People were shaking their heads in disbelief. Susan wanted to leave the sanctuary. She didn't dare look at her husband right then. She figured she'd probably start bawling again if she did catch his eye. She needed to pretend that they were always and forever the "perfect" family.

"Let me read to you from Proverbs," Pastor Bob continued, "Chapter 7 verses 21-27 in the New International Version: With persuasive words she lead him astray; she seduced him with her smooth talk. All at once he followed her like an ox going to the slaughter, like a deer stepping into a noose till an arrow pierces his liver, like a bird darting into a snare, little knowing it will cost him his life."

Pastor Bob paused a moment, looking out into the congregation. Jeff slid his arm around Susan and squeezed her shoulder. She fought back the emotions and sat strong and upright.

Pastor Bob continued reading from Proverbs, "Now then, my sons, listen to me; pay attention to what I say. Do not let your heart turn to her ways or stray into her paths. Many are the victims she has brought down; her slain are a mighty throng. Her house is a highway to the grave, leading down to the chambers of death."

Susan didn't hear another word the rest of the service.

Her inattentiveness did not go unnoticed by the pastor. He planned to call on her that following week. He felt drawn to her. He sensed she was needy.

Max and Hayley drove away, with Susan, Jeff, Natalie and Daniel waving their good byes from the front yard.

"Well, wasn't that a great weekend," Jeff commented. Everyone agreed. Natalie and Daniel were headed to youth group at church and Susan and Jeff returned to the house.

"That was fun," said Susan.

"You are fun," said Jeff.

"Oh yeah," remarked Susan. "A barrel of laughs these days."

"Come here honey," he opened his arms. Susan snuggled in. "I know it may even take years for you to be okay, but it doesn't matter. I'm here for you forever."

They enjoyed a quiet, stress-free rest of the evening together no crying or sadness.

Pastor Bob knocked on Susan's door Monday afternoon. She was surprised.

"Hi," he greeted.

"Hi."

"Just wanted to say how nice it was to see you and your family in church."

"It was nice to be there."

"Could I come in for another visit?"

She stepped back to let him in. Susan felt awkward again.

"I wanted to talk to you about our programs and your interests."

"My interests?"

"Well, you know. See how you want to get involved in our church life and activities."

"Oh."

They sat on the couch. Susan flicked off the TV. She'd had her soaps on.

"You watch soap operas?"

"Yes."

"What ones?"

"Those on CBS."

"So do I when I can."

Susan stared at the pastor. She wasn't expecting that.

"Ministers have time during the week, unlike people in other professions. A lot of us get 'hooked' on daytime viewing. We have lots of meetings and calls we have to make on people during the evening, so it happens." He laughed and his dimples showed up again.

"Neat," she commented. Susan was really not feeling comfortable with a man hanging around, even if he was her new minister. But she was lonely, and wasn't about to be rude, so she tried to relax and enjoy it.

"What do you want to get involved with at church? Sunday School? Choir?"

"At the last church we attended, I counted the money."

"You did?"

"Yes, every Monday."

"That's wonderful. We have a hard time finding people to do bookkeeping kinds of jobs. I'll tell our finance committee." Then he looked like he'd said the wrong thing. "I'm sorry, I'm assuming that you'd be interested."

"That's okay. Go ahead. I need to get involved. It'll be good for me."

"Great!"

Susan wondered if she should offer tea. But then she was nervous about having him hanging around. Those dimples, his kindness, he watches soaps. It didn't seem right or okay.

"Would you like a cup of tea?" She heard herself asking him anyway. All of a sudden she didn't care if it was right or okay.

"I'd love one. And go ahead and turn that TV on. Like I said, I like the soaps, too."

They spent the afternoon watching together.

Chapter 25

Susan's eyes were drawn to the woman at the checkout in the grocery store. It was Jeff's secretary. She wanted to rush to the checkout and pull her hair out at the roots. She wanted to push the woman down and sit on her until she cried. Susan felt such rage.

The woman looked around and noticed Susan. She grabbed her bag and left the store. When Susan had made her purchase, she left the store, too.

"Can I talk to you?" The secretary had waited outside the store for Susan.

"What do you want?" The sight of the woman up close made Susan nauseous. She pictured Jeff seeing the woman naked. It infuriated her.

"I'm so sorry, Susan."

Susan didn't say anything. She only wanted to pummel the woman's face into the parking lot asphalt.

"I am just really sorry. Thank you for forgiving me. I couldn't believe it." Then she leaned in to give Susan a hug. Susan was stiff.

She walked away, leaving Susan standing there in shock.

The hug made her feel further nauseated. Feeling the curves of the woman's body in the hug made her feel sick. Again she imagined her husband seeing and feeling the woman's nakedness. She rushed to her car, afraid of what she might do. She thought she might cry or try to smash her car with her own.

She just cried, and returned home.

Jeff was mowing the lawn when she got there.

Jeff immediately saw that she looked distraught. He stopped the mowing.

"What is it? Are you okay?" He grabbed the grocery bag from the back seat, as Susan got out of the driver's seat.

"I saw her…and it upset me."

"You saw?" Jeff started. "Oh," he then understood.

"Can you believe it? She hugged me?"

"I believe it. She's a bitch."

"It made me sick!"

"She makes me sick!"

"I just wish she'd made you sick back then."

"I know, me, too." Jeff walked her in. When they were inside he set the bag down and held her close. "I know you want this to not be happening, and I'm so sorry it did and it is. If I could kill the woman and get away with it, I would."

"Is she still coming on to you?"

"Absolutely not. She's probably on to someone else. Some poor other idiot like I was."

"She doesn't tempt you?"

"No, I'll never be tempted by another woman as long as I live. You are my baby. You are my life."

"I think I'm going to be okay. But sometimes I don't know."

"You will. And I'm here for you always."

The visits from Pastor Bob were frequent. He usually had some reason for stopping, but after awhile he didn't try to invent one. They watched the soaps and drank tea.

She told Jeff about the more than occasional visits and he looked a little unsure about it, but he'd never been the jealous type, so he didn't say much about it. Still, he knew there was always a possibility that more could develop. After all he knew that first hand.

"As long as you are watching the soaps and not acting them out," he teased, hoping she'd take it okay.

"No, that's your specialty!" she teased back viciously.

"You got me there."

Natalie got a big kick out of the pastor being there when she came home from school one afternoon.

"Hey, Pastor Bob!"

"Hey, Natalie."

They'd taken to each other from the start. After he left, Natalie said, "So is he like our family's friend?"

"I guess so."

"That's cool." Susan thought so, too.

Rachel was busy with canning and cider making, so she was not calling very often. Susan didn't mind because she had Bob dropping by. He'd asked her to call him "Bob." He said they were friends and the "Pastor" part wasn't necessary. Susan thought it odd, but didn't see it as a big deal.

"Could you fill in for our counter at church this week?" he asked after stopping by to visit.

"Sure," Susan responded.

"You'll have to drop by the church office so we can show you how the church does things. Maybe I can take you out to lunch, too."

Susan felt a pang of discomfort. She still wasn't sure about having a guy for a friend, especially one with cute dimples like Bob had. But she heard herself agreeing to it.

"I've had a tough day," Bob said.

"What's the matter?"

They sat on the couch, with the soap AS THE WORLD

TURNS on the TV.

"It's my anniversary. It would have been sixteen years had she lived. It's just hard, still."

"It must be. I'm sorry."

"Her quality of life was so poor at the end. It was awful."

Susan put her hand on his. Their eyes met. "I really am so sorry for you. I bet she was a super gal."

"Yes, she was."

Susan slid her hand off. "If you want to talk about her, I'm a good listener."

"No, no," he said as he got up. "I'd better go."

"Okay." Susan got up, too.

"Don't forget to stop at the church."

"I won't. How about tomorrow?"

"That would be great. Say ten o'clock?"

"Ten o'clock."

She watched him walk out the door. She wondered what he might be like as a love partner. She flushed thinking about such a thing.

It was just so hard to understand why Jeff had done what he'd done. And yet she realized that it was easy to fantasize about someone besides your spouse. "I just did," she confessed. It was the "acting out" of your fantasy that she doubted she could do. But Jeff did it, and that is what had been killing her. And then she remembered an OPRAH show she'd seen and something Oprah had said.

"Forgiveness is a gift you give yourself."

When you've been hurt you sure can use a gift. So "forgiveness" it is. If I never fully understand it, she thought, I could at least live with it. "Forgiveness," a gift you give to yourself. Hmmm.

Puddles

The light that pierces the darkness. The warm breeze that melts the icicles dripping onto your thinking. Forgiveness. The gift you give to yourself. It sounds easy enough, she thought. But is it? She wanted it to be. But wasn't sure.

Chapter 26

Maryann and Beetle were fine, according to the lengthy letter Susan received in the mail. Beetle was doing well in school. Maryann had joined the PTA. And they had a satellite dish sitting in their back yard. Beetle had convinced Maryann that they could get more channels and he'd stay home more if they got one. Susan smiled. Maryann, the parent, she thought. How nice.

Max and Hayley had been to meet her parents, too. Susan wondered how serious they were, but didn't care. All she cared about was that whoever her kids loved, loved them back. And she'd seen first hand that Hayley was smitten with her son.

As for Natalie, she and Daniel were adorable together. They had a healthy teenage relationship. Now, if I could only get my act together, she thought.

Susan believed that Jeff was remorseful about cheating on her, but doubted herself. Her worth. Her sex appeal. Her confidence. That's what cheating does.

That night she dreamt about Bob. Bob and she were dancing. They were holding each other close. She snuggled into the area between his neck and shoulder. Then she awoke. She looked over at Jeff, sleeping soundly beside her. His smell. His touch. That was what she was used to, and that was all that she wanted. She didn't want anyone else. She rolled up behind him. "Hmm," he moaned.

"Mmm," she moaned, too.

Ten o'clock found Susan at the church, waiting for

instructions about counting procedures. Bob came out of his office and looked at Susan. She noticed his eyes gazed downward to her breasts. His gaze stayed a little longer than it should have, but she pretended she didn't notice. Don't want to make a big deal, she thought. After all, the man has been a widower. Maybe it's normal. It did make her feel creepy, though.

"Well, hello."

"Good morning."

"Ready to get indoctrinated?"

"Sure." Susan knew she needed more to do, and church work had always been a nice part of her routine before moving.

They spent an hour and a half going over books and procedures. "Ready to get some lunch?"

"Okay." They left the office and headed for the church parking lot.

"Want me to drive?"

"Well, I should probably follow and then go home from where we eat."

"Don't want to be seen with me?" Bob asked.

"Well, no, I mean," Susan felt embarrassed.

"It's okay," Bob smiled. "That's fine."

She followed his car to a homey-looking diner and parked next to him. They found a vacant table and settled in.

"I'll treat," Bob said. "You are so gracious to help with the counting, it is the least I can do."

"Okay, thanks." Susan looked over the menu and decided on a club sandwich. Bob copied.

"There is a married woman I'm counseling," Bob broke into conversation, "who is having an affair. I'm trying to be nonjudgemental, but that's the hardest part of my job, I find."

"I bet."

"Now take you for example," he said, "I can't imagine that you'd ever have an affair."

"You can't?"

"Of course not."

Susan noticed Bob staring at her face, as if he was trying to take notice of her reaction to his statement.

"You never know about people." Susan's thoughts turned to her Jeff. I never would have thought he would have either, she thought. "So, what do you like about the ministry?" Susan was more than eager to change the subject.

"Meeting people like you." Bob smiled. Dimples prominent and eyes lit up Susan smiled back. It felt good to be appreciated by him.

When he later returned from using the rest room, she caught him staring at her breasts again, but ignored it as she'd done earlier. He's just lonely, she thought.

"Well, thanks for lunch," Susan said after her last bite of food and sip of iced tea.

"How about dessert?"

"No thanks, I have to get going."

"Missing our soaps?"

"No, I have some errands to take care of."

"Thanks for joining me." Bob stood up in a gentlemanly fashion as she left the table.

Chapter 27

Jeff had to attend a conference. Susan was nervous about it. "What is it, dear?" Jeff asked, sensing her nervousness.

Susan remained silent.

"Don't you trust me?"

"I guess I don't."

"That's perfectly understandable. Would you like to go with me?"

"I could?"

"You bet. I'd love it." Jeff whisked Susan around the room. "This will be great!"

"What about Natalie?"

"She can stay with Daniel and Rachel. I'm sure neither would mind."

"Oh, but I just trained to count the money at church."

"You'll have to tell your buddy Bob you can't this time, 'cause you're going with your husband to have wild sex in a hotel!"

Susan laughed. She felt like a newlywed. "You are so bad!"

"And you love me, don't you?"

Susan smiled, paused a few moments and said, "I do. I really do."

Bob did not take the news well when Susan stopped by the church office to tell him.

"But you said you would next time."

Susan was surprised. She'd never seen him angry or

upset in all the visits they'd shared.

"Oh, fine, have a good time!" he snapped at her. This time his gaze fell upon her crotch area, and lasted an uncomfortably long time. Susan felt icky about it, but again pretended not to notice.

He turned away from her and she took the hint to leave.

"I'm sorry. I'll be available after that." She left the office, uncomfortable with his grumping.

On the drive home, she pondered the encounter.

Ministers are only human, she deduced.

She had a marriage to work on, and time away was probably what they needed.

Natalie was ecstatic about staying at Daniel's, as they'd anticipated. Rachel was delighted to have a girl in the house.

Susan packed a variety of clothing for the trip and slipped in a black nylon negligee she'd had in the bottom of her drawer, forgotten about over the years.

They headed for the hotel where the conference was being held, giggling like two newlyweds. "This is wonderful, Sue."

"It is for me, too."

"A new beginning."

Susan smiled. She hated the dark thoughts her husband forced her to think because of what he'd done, but she loved him and was excited about their new beginning, too.

When they got to the room, Jeff grabbed Susan in his arms and threw her on the bed. His mouth sought hers, and his hands grabbed at her buttons like a first-time high school kid excited about making out.

"What are you doing," she asked between forceful kisses.

"I'm ravaging my wife." Jeff's warm breath on her

waiting mouth gave her a rush of warmth where her womanness dwelt. She reached down and tugged at her pants.

"Okay baby." Jeff helped her get them off, then pushed down his own. "Mmm," he moaned.

They usually took their time at lovemaking, but this time was quick and energetic. They came at the same time and collapsed in each other's arms. "Hmm," she groaned.

"You are the sexiest woman alive," Jeff whispered with a husky voice.

"I love you." Susan held him, afraid to think, afraid a dark thought might creep in and spoil their reacquaintance. She loved him so.

"I love you more," Jeff returned. They both laughed softly before relaxing off to sleep for an hour.

The two days away gave Susan a new perspective. She really was going to be okay. She still wanted to tell on "them," but didn't want anyone to ever know about it, either. It was tough, tougher than anything she'd been through, even her parents dying years before. She wondered about counseling. She'd thought about talking to Bob, Pastor Bob, but not after the way he'd acted.

And what about Bob? What was that all about? She didn't know. She thought about leaving Jeff. Maybe she should. What if he did it again? But the thought of leaving him brought the hole back. She hadn't noticed the hole for several months. Had forgotten about it.

Chapter 28

"We're back from the conference," Susan told Bob over the phone. She was feeling guilty about the counting thing.

"Oh, was it a good time?" he asked. She sensed a coolness to his inquiry.

"Yes it was. It's good to get away."

"Great," he remarked, but again she sensed it wasn't genuine or heartfelt.

"I'd be happy to do it next week."

"Oh, that's okay, we're all set."

Susan felt dumb. What was wrong with him? He was so cold.

"Been watching the soaps this week?" she asked.

"Uh, no, not really."

Susan wondered if it was his wife again. Maybe he was depressed. Ministers can get depressed, she thought.

"You want to go out to lunch?" she heard herself asking.

"This time my treat. It's the least I can do for stiffing you after you'd just trained me."

"Okay, where do you want to meet?"

"Let's meet at that diner, I liked that."

"Okay."

She went a few minutes early. She waited for a half-hour and then decided to order. Must be something came up, she thought.

Then he walked in the place.

"Sorry, Susan. A lady called, wanted to talk, I couldn't get off the phone."

"The one who is having the affair?"

"What?"

Susan was embarrassed that she'd said that. "The woman you said you are counseling," she attempted to clarify. "The one who is having an affair?"

"Oh, yeah," he said looking downward, "that's the one."

"No problem, it's your job."

They ate B.L.Ts. Susan did all the talking. Bob was obviously preoccupied, in a bad mood, or both.

"Thanks for lunch," Bob said this time after his last bite and sip of ice tea.

"My pleasure." Susan was ready to leave, too.

After she paid, they walked to the parking lot together. "Have a nice afternoon," she said.

"Oh, you, too." Bob didn't smile or try to say something nice or interesting.

"See ya Sunday," Susan said, wondering if he'd say something about stopping over to watch the soaps, but he didn't.

As he walked away, she wondered again if she could be with another man, say Bob. "Nope, no way," she said aloud. "I'm crazy about one man, my Jeff."

Jeff came home anxious to chat about his day. "The best thing happened today, Sue!"

"Tell me," she begged. "What is it?"

"The bitch resigned!"

"What?"

"She resigned!"

Susan felt faint. She wanted to trust Jeff, felt she could,

knew why he didn't dare fire her, but wanted her gone in the worst way.

"Tell me about it."

"She handed in her resignation, told me she has a boyfriend who is a CEO with some big corporation and he got transferred out of state so she's going with him."

"I hope he's married and she gets dumped!"

"Susan, you are so bad."

"And I'm so good," she looked sexy and suggestive.

"That you are, my little sex kitten. I love you so."

Susan put her arms around him and hugged him tightly.

"I'm so sorry," Jeff burst into tears.

Susan stepped back. "What is this about?"

"I'm just so sorry for hurting you so bad."

She returned to hugging him. "I forgive you, honey."

"You are so wonderful, Sue. I'm the luckiest man alive."

Chapter 29

It was a beautiful sun shiny day for Natalie's birthday. Max and Hayley were driving up for the party. Maryann and Beetle were invited, too. And Rachel, Daniel, Jen, Shana, and Pastor Bob were also expected.

Susan and Natalie were busy blowing up balloons for decorating, and Jeff was cleaning the patio where he would grill hot dogs and hamburgers.

"I can't believe I love it here so much," Natalie commented.

"I'm so grateful," Susan said.

"I can't believe I thought I loved Johnny."

"Oh?"

"Yeah. I mean Daniel is much more mature and together than Johnny ever thought he was."

"Does that mean you think you love Daniel?"

"I don't know," Natalie tied the end of the balloon she'd just inflated. "I know he makes me feel wonderful. He's nice and fun and," she laughed. "I guess I do."

"You are so cute these days," her mother laughed, too.

"A lot better than Miss Moody."

"You got that right."

They finished the last of the balloons when Jeff walked into the room.

"How are my girls doing?"

"Great!" answered Susan.

"Look at all the balloons we blew up, Dad."

"Wow! I always knew you two were full of hot air."

Natalie playfully slapped her father on the arm.

They began to tape the balloons up around the room to make it look festive. They were all orange and red, Natalie's favorite colors. Natalie had even painted her room orange. Jeff and Susan had not been thrilled, but it was her room and they really didn't care that much. At least she was happy and positive these days, they thought. They were thankful for that.

"Our little girl is sixteen," Jeff said. "Can you believe it, Mother?"

"Yes, and no," she smiled.

"Yes and no?" Natalie looked puzzled.

"Sometimes it seems like only yesterday that you were born and other times it has seemed like I've been raising you for centuries," Susan laughed.

"Oh great, Mom," Natalie rolled her eyes.

"Just kidding," Susan teased. "Gotcha!"

Max and Hayley walked in next.

"Hey! It looks like a party!" Max greeted his family.

They all dropped what they were doing to return the greeting. Hugs went all around, with Hayley, too.

Next, Maryann and Beetle rang the doorbell. Beetle had grown several inches since they'd moved away. Everyone commented.

"Must be Maryann's home cooking," Susan teased.

"Now, now," Maryann responded. "I am using a Betty Crocker Cook Book these days and I'm getting pretty good, aren't I Beetle?"

"You bet you are. We had chicken and dumplings last night. They were awesome."

"Well, hey they were awesome,' which means you are 'A-okay," Jeff remarked.

Daniel, Rachel, Jen and Shana arrived next. Introductions went all around. Punch was served up and chips and pretzels were munched on as everyone mingled.

Rachel approached Susan. "I don't know whether or not Pastor Bob is going to make it."

"Oh," Susan said.

"He called me and asked for a ride, then called and said to tell you he might not be able to make it."

"Oh well."

"He's been acting kind of down, lately. I think he misses his wife more than he realizes."

"You are probably right," agreed Susan. "That's too bad."

The next two hours were filled with eating, laughing, and candles and birthday cake. Natalie saved opening presents for last.

"Boy, you know she's growing up. It used to be that she'd beg to open her presents first thing." Susan's comment made everyone laugh, even Natalie.

Maryann tugged on Susan's sleeve. Susan smiled at her. "Looks like you guys are getting along great," she whispered.

"We sure are," Susan whispered back. "We sure are."

Susan worried about Bob. She was drawn to him like a mother to a hurting child. He'd been a good pal, coming over and hanging out, and now she had a feeling that he was the one who needed a friend. She called him up the next morning.

"I'm sorry you couldn't make it to Natalie's party," Susan said.

"Oh yeah, I'm really sorry," he said, "something came up."

"No problem. We missed you."

"Well, thanks."

There was a long pause.

"Would you like to meet for lunch?" Susan asked.

"I can't," he said, "thanks, though."

"Okay," Susan didn't know what else to say. "Have a nice day."

"You, too."

They hung up and Susan became more and more curious about Bob.

She called Rachel next.

"I see what you mean about Bob, I mean Pastor Bob."

"Isn't he sad sounding?" Rachel said.

"Yes, I wonder what's going on with him. He's usually so smiley and enthusiastic."

"Oh, so you've noticed his dimples, too?"

Susan blushed, and said, "Yes, I have."

"He used to come over frequently, and then stopped visiting all of a sudden."

"Same here," Susan found that very interesting.

"Hmm. Oh well, he's a good man. Maybe it's nothing."

"Well, it's given us something to talk about," Susan joked.

"You've got a point there."

"Well, I won't keep you. I know you have lots to do around the farm."

"Thanks for inviting us to the party. We had a lovely time."

"I'm glad you did."

Susan was curious, so she set out to do a little investigation on Bob. She remembered how the investigation with Jill, Maryann's old friend, had gone, but nonetheless, she was on a mission.

She drove to the church, thought she'd drop in, pretend to have questions about counting.

When she got to the corner of the intersection where the church was located, she saw Bob outside the church talking to a woman. The woman was attractive; she'd noticed her at church before. They seemed very intense.

Susan turned around the corner out of sight. She figured she'd drive around awhile and then try again. She imagined that this was the woman he'd been counseling. Maybe he was telling her to go back to her husband, and stop the affair.

"I watch the soaps too much," she mocked herself out.

After ten minutes of riding, she drove back to the church. They were still out there, still talking, still looking intense. This time Bob spun around, dramatically and spotted Susan in her car. He stood there staring. She waved. He waved back.

Susan drove up with the car. She felt awkward, but thought it would look stupid if she drove the other way again.

"Hi Susan, what's up?" Bob greeted.

"Just thought I'd stop in to see if you need me to count next week. I was driving in the neighborhood, and you know."

"Sure, well, I don't think we do, but thanks."

Susan noticed the woman looked their way. Susan felt like she was interrupting, so she said good bye and left.

Chapter 30

The soaps couldn't keep her interest that afternoon. They seemed dull. "Maybe I'm the one who is dull," she said out loud. She got out a crossword puzzle to work on. That occupied her mind until it was time to start preparing dinner. She worked on frying ham slices, boiling potatoes for mashed potatoes, and putting together a salad. "Can't forget pineapple slices, we always have pineapple slices with ham." Susan smiled at the idea of her talking to herself.

Natalie was staying at Jen's after school to work on homework. Jeff came through the door whistling. "What are you whistling about?"

"I'm just the luckiest guy on the planet."

"Oh yeah? Why is that?"

"Because I'm married to the most fabulous woman in the Universe!"

"Well the most fabulous woman was a bit sneaky today."

"What now?" Jeff teased.

"I did a little snooping."

"Uh oh."

Susan proceeded to fill Jeff in on Rachel's call about Bob and her drive to the church.

"Maybe he could use a male friend. Would you like me to call him?"

"Well, sure. He is our family friend, as Natalie puts it."

"More like your friend," Jeff rolled his eyes at his wife."

"Well, you had your little fling, I can have mine, can't I?"

Jeff chased her around the kitchen. "Pastor Bob?"

Susan let herself be caught.

They wrestled a few minutes before settling into each other's arms. The potato water boiled over just as they kissed.

"Rain check Tiger!" Susan pulled away. She raced for the stove, took the lid off the pot, and turned down the heat.

"Pastor Bob?"

"Yes?"

"This is Jeff. I wondered if you'd want to stop by my office someday. You know, get to know each other better. Maybe talk about the youth programs at church."

"Well, um, I'm pretty busy this week, maybe next week."

"Okay, have a good night."

Jeff looked at Susan as he hung up the phone. "Your buddy couldn't get off the phone fast enough."

"Oh really."

"Hmm."

"Rachel thinks he may be missing his wife."

"His wife?"

"She died a few years ago."

"Maybe that's it. Well, at least we tried."

"Thanks hon."

Max and Hayley wanted to tell their parents, but thought they'd better wait. They had one more year before they'd both earn their Associates Degree, and why give their parents anything to be concerned about? The fact that they'd decided to become engaged was a big deal to them and they didn't want to take the chance that any of their parents might object or not be as thrilled as they were about it.

They were sexually involved, but using protection, so they felt like they were acting maturely, and responsibly. So they'd wait. "We'll tell them at graduation next year," said Max.

"I don't know if I can hold off. I love you too much not to want to scream it to the world."

"I love you too much, too, Hayley."

Natalie and Daniel were teenage goofy and everyone loved it.

"If they want to jump in puddles I surely won't care," said Susan to Jeff one evening when they were watching the teens trying to climb a tree in the yard.

"Whatever are you talking about?"

"Oh, that's right, you were away." Susan filled him in on the time when she was intolerant of their daughter's jumping in puddles.

"You are really loosening up, old girl!" Jeff smacked her on the bottom.

"Hey, watch it, freshie!"

"Freshie is right, I want to get fresh with you, baby!"

"Those two are adorable, and to think about how upset I was about her and Johnny. It's nice to be relaxed about her and Daniel."

"You mean you don't think they'd ever fool around?"

"I'm relaxed, not stupid. Those farm boys, you know..."

Jeff grinned. He loved being back to joking with his best friend, his wife, his lover. Nothing made him happier.

Just then Natalie fell off a low branch and into Daniel's arms.

"Hmm, big Daniel mighty strong," mocked Jeff.

"You used to do cute caveman stuff like that to me,

too."

"Well, let's go snuggle on the couch, before the young lovebirds try to claim it. You want me to drag you by the hair, caveman style?"

"No, to the hair dragging. Yes, to the snuggling."

Bob paced restlessly. He thought about stopping by to talk to Jeff. Maybe I should, he thought. "I just don't know."

Chapter 31

They needed volunteers at school, and Jeff's new secretary asked if he thought Susan might be interested. "I bet she would be. Go ahead and call her."

His new secretary was pleasant, efficient, and seemed totally trustworthy. She called Susan right up.

"You could file or read to students, there's a number of jobs that need doing."

"I'd love to." Susan was thrilled to be included. She was to begin the next week. "Life is good," she thought. How I could feel so low, almost suicidal before, and feel this good now is incredible, she thought.

In an inspirational moment, Susan decided to try to be a more thankful person. "Thank you Lord for my wonderful life."

She opened up the King James Bible they kept on the shelf in the living room and flipped through until she got to the Twenty-third Psalm:

"The Lord is my shepherd; I shall not want. He maketh me to lie down in green pastures: he leadeth me beside the still waters. He restoreth my soul: he leadeth me in the paths of righteousness for his name's sake. Yea though I walk through the valley of the shadow of death, I will fear no evil: for thou art with me; thy rod and thy staff they comfort me. Thou preparest a table before me in the presence of my enemies: thou annointest my head with oil; my cup runneth over. Surely goodness and mercy shall follow me all the days of my life: and

I will dwell in the house of the Lord forever."

Susan read slowly, trying to take in each word and discern its meaning for her. She ended by crying soft tears of hope.

Church was an activity they still looked forward to as a family. They especially loved the way Pastor Bob performed the service. So when the pastor was not at church, they were disappointed, which was the case the next Sunday.

A member of the committee that deals with concerns about the pastor stood up with a sheet of paper in her hand and read the following:

"It is with shame and because of human weakness that I confess that I have not behaved appropriately as your pastor and I therefore have resigned, signed Pastor Bob."

The congregation looked around at each other in shock. A woman wailed as if a close relative had died. Susan looked at Jeff. "Wow," he mouthed. No further explanation was offered. A lay person conducted the service.

After the service there was lots of talk in the church parking lot. Many women were crying. Many were consoling. Rachel approached the family. She took Susan aside.

"Are you okay?"

"Well, yes," she answered. "I don't understand, but I'm okay."

"I guess he had a pattern," explained Rachel, "from what I understand. He'd stop by to visit women in the congregation during the day and sometimes something more than a friendship would develop. This time a husband caught him with his wife. And Pastor Bob and the woman took off together."

Susan was struck dumb.

"Pretty shocking, huh?"

"He came to my house many times." Then Susan looked at Rachel. "Nothing happened."

Rachel smiled. "I know, he used to come to my house, too."

"You just never know, do you?"

"And we were worried about him missing his dead wife?"

At that they both laughed.

"I've even heard that he did the same thing at another church, even when his wife was alive. Now I'm not sure, but like I said, it's supposedly a pattern with him."

"Boy, and they say soap operas are far fetched. Life is a soap opera, I'm beginning to believe."

"You could be right," Rachel smiled.

Susan filled in Natalie and Jeff after she got into the car with them.

"That is disgusting!" Natalie said. "Grownups having affairs! That makes me sick!"

Jeff looked uncomfortable, while Susan felt as if she'd won some kind of victory, achieved some kind of accomplishment, overcome something she thought was insurmountable. The children never had to know. She was okay with that.

Chapter 32

The engagement party was held at Hayley's house. Everyone wore white, at the bride-to-be's request. There were gold and silver streamers winding around the banister and fresh flowers in vases all around the room. Hayley's parents were delighted. They adored Max. No one had a problem with the mixed race issue, and the parents all got along great.

Natalie brought Daniel to the get together. Susan and Jeff were arm and arm. Their son was going to be married as soon as the couple secured jobs. Max had an interview the following week.

"Where did our little boy go?" Jeff whispered.

"He's quite the man, now," Susan whispered back.

Hayley approached them. "Congratulations," they greeted.

"Thank you," she laughed softly. "I'm going to make your son very happy."

"You already do, my dear."

"Do you have any mother-in-law advice for me?" she laughed again.

"Hmm," Susan thought for a moment. Her mind floated to a cloud of memory involving her mother. Her mother's favorite bible passages were from the King James version of I Corinthians 13.

She remembered her mother saying: (I Corinthians 13:13) "And now abide faith, hope, love, these three; but the greatest of these is love."

She looked at Jeff, then looked back at Hayley and said, "Love each other."

"That's it?" Hayley looked surprised.

"That's it." Susan hugged her.